The patterns on Foundry Editions' covers have been designed to capture the visual heritage of the Mediterranean. This one is inspired by classic twentieth-century Italian design. It was created by Hélène Marchal.

CHIARA VALERIO was born in Scauri in 1978 and lives in Rome. She has published essays, novels, and short stories, including *La gioia piccola d'esser quasi salvi* (2009), *Spiaggia libera tutti* (2010), *Il cuore non si vede* (2019), *La matematica è politica* (2020), *Nessuna scuola mi consola* (2021), *Così per sempre* (2022) and *La tecnologia è religione* (2023).

AILSA WOOD is a translator from Italian and French. Her work on Stefano Benni's monologues from *Le Beatrici* (2021) was the winner of the prestigious John Dryden Translation Competition in 2022. Besides her work as a literary translator, she works across various related sectors, including wine and tourism. Ailsa has an MA in Literary Translation from the University of East Anglia and lives in Italy.

PRAISE FOR *THE LITTLE I KNEW*

"Enigmatic and beguiling, precise and unsettling, this seductive novel opens with a mysterious death, asking compelling questions about desire, knowability and the still limited possibilities of freedom for women. Chiara Valerio is a major talent, and she makes the small town of Scauri, between Rome and Naples, a place of fascination."

—OLIVIA LAING

"With wit, subtlety and charm, Valerio captures the complex currents of secrecy and desire that is just under the surface of small-town and family life. A beguiling, atmospheric story of female fascinations."

—SARAH WATERS

"The writing is nimble and on point. The structure is tight, with a death at the beginning that brings to mind Ginzburg or Sciascia. Chiara Valerio tells the story of what remains of small-town life, if that's what we can still call it."

—JHUMPA LAHIRI

"With an elegance that races, Chiara Valerio tells the story of Scauri, a city that appears to be dead, but that is truly alive. A city full of mysteries and everyday, bittersweet pleasures. The narrative is an enchantment of phantasmagorical goings-on and the small realities of provincial life."

—DACIA MARAINI

"In the story Chiara Valerio tells, there is something of the relationship between Vita Sackville-West and Virginia Woolf, something of that elegance and of those gardens, of gentle slowness and ancient bonds."

—VALERIA PARRELLA IN *GRAZIA*

"Chiara Valerio plays with the noir genre and transforms it; rather she reveals what is at its heart. Yes of course we need to find out how Vittoria died. But maybe it's more crucial to find out how Vittoria lived."

—PAOLO DI PAOLO IN *LA REPUBBLICA*

THE LITTLE I KNEW

CHIARA VALERIO

The Little
I Knew

Translation by Ailsa Wood

**FOUNDRY
EDITIONS**

The truth is that by making collections of things, plants, everything, we end up gradually wanting to collect people, too.
MICOL FINZI-CONTINI

No one is able to control themselves perfectly.
TERESA CREMISI, *La triomphante*

The girls got out of the car and ran off, without saying goodbye to us. My mother, standing in the doorway, hugged them and smiled at me, lifting her chin as if to say Don't worry.

Luigi started up the car before I could regret it or change my mind about accepting the invitation to spend a weekend on Ponza, in a house overlooking the port.

The ferry crossing from Formia was pleasant and Friday afternoon was hot. Hot and humid. And the air was heavy on Saturday and Sunday morning, before we left, as if it might rain, but it didn't. We walked, ate, and swam. Luigi didn't, he said the water was cold. Although that wasn't true. He just preferred to listen to the chatter, sitting at one of the tables at the bar in the port.

On Sunday evening, when we got home, I put the girls to bed, flicked through the afternoon edition of *Il Golfo*, the photocopied bulletin for the two parishes, and smoked a cigarette.

If I didn't see the news of Vittoria's death, it was because I don't read the obituaries and property ads before going to bed.

On Monday morning, while I was in my office trying to persuade the ironmonger and his wife not to sue after their son had come off worst in a fight, my secretary Cristina came into the room to tell me there was a woman on the phone, insisting on speaking to me. I stood up and excused myself to get some privacy.

It was Mara. Vittoria died yesterday morning, she said in a flat, calm tone, a courtesy call. I know she liked you, and you liked her.

She'd called their other friends too.

I couldn't think of anything to ask her. I thought of myself, alive, in Ponza while Vittoria was dying in Scauri.

An accident, Mara explained. An accident in the bath, she repeated, her voice faltering after every syllable. I assured her I would go and see her and, without thanking me, she said She's here at home, the funeral's the day after tomorrow, before ending the call.

I went back into the office and carried on talking to the ironmonger and his wife, keeping my eyes on the keyhole which occasionally appeared in the door behind their heads, which were bobbing back and forth in the heat of their story. He was almost shouting, he seemed to have taken it badly that his son had been beaten up.

Lea, that lad threw a beer bottle at him, and thank God it didn't hit him in the head, it would've killed him, but it just grazed him, see? Riccardo's not a chicken, so he went over and punched him, and the other lad dodged, headbutted him, and broke his nose. It wasn't an accident.

It wasn't an accident, repeated Anna, the boy's mother. You have to stop this kind of behaviour while you can, she added, turning around suddenly, annoyed, perhaps to see what I was staring at past her head.

An accident in the bath, I thought, and I saw Vittoria again with her swaying walk, her intense eyes, neither light nor dark, the pale-blue sleeveless linen dress she wore. I saw her walking along the pavement, stopping in front of shop windows and shaking her head. What she felt about the objects she saw there, I never knew. She used to enjoy talking about things you couldn't, or shouldn't, laugh at. People who cheated on each other. People who built two-family vaults at the top of the cemetery. People who tripped over. Wheelchair users blocked by architectural barriers. Can you imagine? Nothing but barriers, for sure.

I knew that bathtub she died in, I'd been to Vittoria's house many times. You couldn't miss it because the front door, which gave onto a long corridor, was opposite the bathroom, and at the far end there was the bath, under a window with yellow and green panes, an irregular chequered pattern of squares and rectangles, while the floor and walls were shiny black tiles.

The house had been renovated in the early seventies, when Vittoria moved to Scauri to live with Mara. We all knew that bathtub, and of course we'd noticed it because of those black tiles. So Enrico told me, anyway. I'd asked him about it for some reason, perhaps when we had the work done on our house. Enrico supplied bathroom fittings and tiles across the Sud Pontino area beyond Fondi, and he was my husband's uncle. I was sure no one had ever lived in that house before, as far as I could remember.

Since Vittoria had come, it was always open. You came in through the garden and there'd be a cheery atmosphere on the patio, people chatting, dogs chasing each other, cats jumping on the tables and sharpening their claws on the trees. There was a peacock, too, Patrick.

From the first time I went there, that's what it was always like. For me, and for everyone else, because before they even finished sorting out the house they had a party, for Mara's birthday. I wasn't there, I was told about it. Everyone had talked about it.

A little building, with a few fancy flourishes, but rundown, ground floor and first floor, with a lovely entrance, in Via Romanelli, and a little garden that had flourished over twenty years. Vittoria knew about herbs, she read about gardens and walked a lot, she could walk as far as the Redeemer, where the statue of Christ was. Reading about gardens was very unusual, too, according to the bookshop where Vittoria ordered her manuals. Unusual in the sense of strange. After all, we had vegetable patches and flower beds – gardens were for posh people's houses. Or belonged to the council. General Nobile's villa had a garden, and so did the municipal villa, a public garden with merry-go-rounds behind the Sayonara ice cream shop.

When they arrived no one asked too many questions, perhaps because no one realised they were going to stay. Vittoria started working in the pharmacy, Mara opened a cat and dog boarding and grooming business before anyone else had thought of it. I don't even know whether it was a legal business, or what its tax situation was, but lots of people went there, out of curiosity or because, sooner or later, everyone needs someone to look after their dog or cat for a few days.

So I dropped in myself, in December 1974.

I'd argued with my mother and I didn't want to ask her to look after my dog, Madama. Mum wouldn't accept that the days were gone when dogs and cats were either strays you gave a bit of food from time to time – only a bit, you mustn't let them get fond of you – and who risked getting run over every single day, or animated brooms or hoes: work tools. Dogs kept guard and cats caught mice, chickens laid eggs, cows provided milk and meat, pigs were slaughtered once a year, and my job was to wash the innards to be stuffed with sausage and salami meat. The idea of pets for company never crossed her mind. If it doesn't talk, what sort of company's that? Mum would protest curtly, sweeping the kitchen floor. I was a tool to her too and, as I was a girl, I was to be her walking stick in old age. An animated stick. She didn't even want me to accept the scholarship after university. Lea, get to work, you've got to get yourself married.

Mum would have left Madama outside the house for those three days. I didn't want to get married, I wanted to go on studying and run off for a couple of days to see Luigi, who was doing his military service, but I didn't know where to leave the dog, so my best friend Alba suggested Mara's pet boarding service. She'd never been there, but she'd heard about it on the train to Rome. That way you don't need to worry, otherwise you'll be thinking about Madama when you're with Luigi. Alba's always been a practical woman.

I liked Luigi, he called Madama a fake wolf, he was an army reserve officer in some far-flung place outside of Salerno, the Snake Pit.

The garden of the house where Mara and Vittoria lived wasn't beautiful like it is now. The roof was yet to be a roof terrace, there were no railings, but you could see someone cared about it and had started looking after it on a daily basis. In a few months, everything was on the way to flourishing. The pet boarding and grooming business wasn't fashionable, vets mostly looked after chickens and sheep, cows and pigs, occasionally rabbits. Rabbits are particularly delicate.

The Redeemer, where Vittoria picked plants and flowers which she later transplanted at sea level, was a peak of the

Aurunci Mountains, Monte Altino, known as the Redeemer because of the statue of Christ.

It was clear they'd come to stay because the owner of the pharmacy, a very distinguished woman from Livorno, heard from a friend that Vittoria hadn't rented but purchased the house in Via Romanelli, and that Mara wasn't her daughter, even though Vittoria had registered the property in her name. The notary had said so one morning in Bar Italia while commenting on another inheritance case that had tickled him, concerning a house in Vindicio for which it had been complicated to find even one heir, a lovely house, and in the end the heir had turned it down in favour of a friend of the uncle who owned it. But what kind of friend, no one could say. The name Vindicio immediately brought to mind the name Formia, which immediately ignited a sense of local rivalry in the hearts of the people of Scauri against that town less than ten kilometres to the north. Perhaps that was why this juicy morsel of information about Mara not being the daughter had generated no gossip but had remained like karst. Water running under the town's feet, like the Capo d'Acqua river, which had been buried, with only short sections visible from the Parco delle Trote as far as the sea. And in those short sections children collected tadpoles, sealing them in jam jars. Sometimes the tadpoles were set free into the stream and became frogs, but more often they died.

On the Madama day, a woman with dark hair just above her shoulders saw me outside the gate with an elderly dog and came over to me, smiling. With a quick, firm jerk of her head she freed her right eye from a lock of hair. Her sparkly eyes were neither light nor dark, and she wore a straw hat that had seen better days, loose trousers, and a white cable-knit jumper, and was clutching a pair of shears. My mother also worked the land, and had a certain elegance, but Vittoria looked like she had stepped out of the pages of *Oggi*, where I occasionally read articles about exiled royals. She looked like an Arabian princess on a Tuscan country estate. Except that behind her there was the shabby little building. An untidy garden and cracked plaster. It had belonged to the Nocellas, who owned all the land from the Via Appia to the railway before the business about the horse.

I wondered if it would be possible to leave her the dog for a couple of days, and how much it would cost. That's what I said, without even a polite good morning.

Vittoria kept smiling and answered Come in and sit down, anyway. Would you like a glass of water, a coffee? A tamarind cordial?

Without waiting for an answer she laid a hand on my arm, then set off towards the front door, left the shears on a little metal table, and went inside, taking off her hat. Her hair was smartly cut but windswept. On the patio there was a table with two chairs. She turned in the doorway as if to focus on me, tilted her head. I looked away, blushing, examined my jumper in search of a stain.

A few minutes later she came out, accompanied by two girls, put her hat back on, and made a polite gesture, touching the brim with her fingertips, then went back to where I had found her. There was something martial about her. A martial courtesy, and something bobbing, billowy, a ship's captain.

My grandfather would tip his hat as a sign of respect or farewell. After taking the oath, Luigi had sent me a photo in his officer's uniform, with a peaked hat. You could tell he had blue eyes even in black and white. I've always liked blue eyes. I think the first thing I loved about Luigi was his blue-green eyes. Men usually doff their hats.

I knew one of the two girls. Filomena had been in my class at primary school, she was the undertaker's daughter. When she saw me, she didn't acknowledge me – after all, we hadn't hung out together since. I'd never seen the other one before, she looked like a doll. Blonde hair in braids long enough to wind twice around her head. She was wearing a pair of faded flared jeans, a very brightly coloured shirt, and rectangular tortoiseshell-framed glasses. She put her hands close to Madama's muzzle.

Hi, I'm Mara. Is she a friendly girl, this one? she said.

Yes, she's friendly, but a bit incontinent, I answered quickly, then turned to Filomena, who was pretending not to recognise me, or so it seemed to me.

It's me, Lea, remember?

Yes, yes, we were at primary school together. But you were a good girl, Le', I've never seen you down at the beach club since. She burst out laughing.

I went to the cliffs with my older brother instead.

But I haven't seen you out and about since then, either.

Perhaps we had different timetables. I went to liceo in Formia, then university in Naples. Buses, trains, studying, and helping my mum at home, you know.

I said you were a good girl. What are you doing now?

The bar exam.

Madonna, you've already got a degree, aren't you getting married?

I don't know why, but before I answered, I looked at Vittoria, who had turned her attention away from the leaves and was now staring at me curiously. Her hands were raised above her head, one holding up a branch, the other pruning. Climbing roses, she said, raising her voice, they're hardy but you have to give them a direction, otherwise they just grow in a bush.

Yes, Filomena, I've got a boyfriend, but there's plenty of time to get married. At present I'm going back and forth to Rome, I won a scholarship at the Pro Deo.

I lowered my eyes and met Madama's, who was watching me, tongue hanging out, asking my permission to move away. She looked from me and then to a dog lying under a tree, three or four times.

It'll be three hundred lire a day, said Mara, food, board, and brushes, you can leave her now if you want, she doesn't seem to want to run away. And she laughed. Not coarsely, like Filomena, but a crystal clear sound, the stream in the trout park up there at Monte d'Oro, when the fish were jumping. A freshwater fish farm in a seaside town. There was a pool too, with slides. And a bar and restaurant.

Three hundred lire was a lot, but I could afford it, and I wanted to prove to my mum that I was independent, at least financially, and to spite her as well.

Farmed fish jump too, Luigi had told me the day before he left for his military service. Then he'd kissed me. And his moustache hadn't bothered me. There had been an accident in the pool at Parco delle Trote. A boy ended up paralysed. Pools are empty in winter. Are bushes ugly?

It was an accident, too, that lost the Nocellas their land and houses. The horse had kicked the patriarch, killing him, and the wife was left with seven children and had to sell everything, bit by bit. Lucky they had something to sell, some people don't even have that, they'd mutter down at the fishermen's houses near the cliffs. Some people only have themselves to sell, and that isn't enough to live on.

An accident in the bathtub, I kept hearing, like a radio left on, while I was waiting for my pizza order at Lu Rusticone. We had pizza for dinner on Mondays. An accident in the bathtub, repeated in the streets.

Avvocato Russo, did you hear about Vittoria? An accident in the bathtub.

Carmela, who worked at Ernesto Bruno, the haberdashery opposite Lu Rusticone, gave me an enquiring look, but I had nothing to tell her except about the phone call that morning.

Yes, an accident in the bath, I heard myself repeat, and then went on, Mara rang me this morning to tell me, I was out yesterday, the funeral's on Wednesday.

Just think, avvoca', I only bumped into Vittoria yesterday morning, at the cliffs, and she jumped in as usual and swam for at least half an hour, it might have been seven, or quarter past. You know, avvoca', at one point I thought she'd drowned, she wasn't coming back, then I saw her past the buoy, and she even waved, and when she came back up she said she'd stopped at the Madonnina to look at Ischia.

Could you see Ischia on Sunday morning?

Mondragone and Ponza as well, it was clear, like a magnifying glass.

And then what?

Then nothing, avvoca', we had a coffee at Lo Scoglio, and waited till our hair dried a bit. She was happy, joking around like always, she said You know, Carmela, every day should be like today. Like what? I asked her, because we'd only talked about the fight with the bottles the night before, but she didn't answer, she took off her shoes, perhaps there was some sand in them, banged them on the table leg, and left the money for the coffee. And then never mind the sea, she drowned in her own bath, avvoca'. Anyway, do you know anything about those two who were fighting?

Yes, Riccardo's parents came to press charges, Riccardo's got a broken nose.

They want money, avvoca', that Riccardo's daft as a brush.

Sorry, Carmela, it's my turn and the girls are waiting for me.

I'm sorry, avvoca', have a good evening, and say hello to the Prof. The ironmonger's son's rough, remember that trouble at Easter, avvoca'.

Every day should be like today, I repeated to myself, wondering Like what? What had Vittoria meant? Luigi, who appeared uninterested in town life but knew everything, had told me Mara wasn't home when Vittoria came back on Sunday, she'd gone to walk Councillor Comi's two Great Danes. Mara had walked as far as Spigno, via Santa Maria, then she'd been tired and hitch-hiked, and come back with someone from the gas bottle shop at the top of the hill. When she went to the bathroom to wash her hands, she found Vittoria under the water, she hadn't seen her from the corridor, you see? But she didn't scream, she lifted her up and kissed her.

Sorry, how do you know that?

We both turned to make sure the girls, who listened to everything and repeated everything they heard, really were distracted by the pizza.

How do you know, Luigi?

From Franca, you know she goes to clean at theirs after eleven o'clock Mass on Sundays. She'd just put down her bag in the hall and she saw it all. She went over and when she saw what had happened, she started screaming. That's when they called the ambulance, but obviously it was too late to do anything.

But how did it happen?

She drowned in the bath.

Was there an autopsy?

Of course. Tommaso did it, and he found water in her lungs.

But how can that be?

I don't know, Lea, it was a terrible accident. Franca swore that from the entrance, with the bathroom door framing the scene, it looked like the prince kissing Snow White. You know, she's got young grandchildren, and now all she watches is cartoons.

The girls had eaten all the pizza while they watched *Bedknobs and Broomsticks*. They hadn't washed their hands. The greasy little fingerprints on the pleather sofa smelt of the pizza I hadn't eaten. Since the video recorder had come along, they asked for videocassettes instead of toys. Luigi had the knack of buying toys for himself that the children saw as toys for them. Scientists lead children's lives. We collected the videos that came with *L'Unità* and *La Repubblica*. Classic films. Westerns. Later, locked in the bathroom, smoking, I looked at the bathtub. Sitting on the edge, I scanned the bottom as if it might reveal what happened to Vittoria. How does an expert swimmer, someone who dives into the sea in winter and summer, die by drowning in her own bathtub? An accident, avvocato. A terrible tragedy, Lea. Every day should be like today.

I opened the previous evening's *Il Golfo*, looking for what I should have seen and hadn't, and read: Our friend Vittoria has had an accident in her home. Perhaps a fall, perhaps a tragic accident. We grieve for her together, now and forever.

Accident, again.

Would the yellow non-slip fish protect the girls?

The next day, Angelo, the ironmonger, was waiting for me in the office. He told me he was worried about Riccardo, because they were already calling him The Ram down in the square. Well, what do you expect, if you're the one on the receiving end of the headbutt? Angelo handed over a blurry, unfocused Polaroid that showed someone throwing something on the beach. It did actually look like a bottle. I recognised the blue beach umbrellas of the Lido Oriente, closed and secretive like buds, and the breakwaters in front of the beach. A person with short, blonde, curly hair, in a T-shirt and shorts, feasibly a boy, even more feasibly Riccardo.

The photo had been taken by someone standing behind him, and the person throwing the bottle stood opposite. An unrecognisable, regular-featured face, a light-coloured polo shirt, with a blue jumper around the shoulders, long trousers, probably loafers, but you couldn't see them, the feet were cut off.

He's the one who started it, you can tell. Angelo was talking but I wasn't listening. In the distance, at the water's edge, was Vittoria, an evening shadow, less blurry than the rest, caught midstep: her usual swaying walk, a sleeveless dress, a shirt tied sash-like around her waist; her hair, which had been white for a few years and suited her, her head high; something in front of her face, probably her glasses – she used to take them off and put one of the arms in her mouth, dangling them from the tip between her teeth. She did it often. She'd never dyed her hair and, when I looked at her, I thought I would do the same.

What time was it? I asked The Ram's dad.

Before dinner, eight, half eight, do you need the photo, avvoca'?

Who took it?

One of my son's friends, he had the Polaroid camera for his birthday, but his pictures are always out of focus, he's a muppet.

I don't think I'll need it, but leave it with me. Are you sure you want to go ahead and press charges? They're both minors.

Avvocato Russo, I'm a father, I don't want Riccardo to grow up with the idea that you can hit people or get hit without consequences.

Angelo, let me be clear that the direction we're taking will leave a minor, perhaps several minors, with criminal records.

Lea, the boy that chucked the bottle's from Rome, these kids can't come here, throwing their weight around in their loafers. What real man wears loafers anyway? Come on, it's like a man eating strawberry ice cream. They think they can get away with it even when someone might have been seriously hurt, not just a broken nose. Anyway, I'll ask my wife. But seriously, avvoca', has it ever crossed your mind to throw a bottle at someone?

When Angelo had gone, I rang Luigi's school – he only had two hours on Tuesdays and then he stayed in the lab. I was sure he'd know all about the Easter trouble Carmela had mentioned the previous evening while we were queuing for pizza. And sure enough, that gossip of a husband of mine knew everything, as usual.

There had actually been two Easter troubles.

Riccardo had gone into the sacristy with his cousins Andrea, six, and Alessandra, eight, because Father Michele had recently stocked up the church's wine. The plan was to steal a few bottles and get drunk with his friends at the Sieci, near the furnace chimney. Distracted by the opportunity to grab a few unconsecrated communion wafers, he left his cousins and went searching for some kind of bag or a pillowcase for the purpose, exploring the little rooms of the rectory, which was full of wine tapped off into Coca-Cola bottles. The two children drank just enough alcohol not to alarm Riccardo but enough to be found a few hours later in the rabbit hutch, biting the rabbits' ears. The rabbits were distressed, the cousins spilled the beans, and Riccardo had to give back the wine and serve at Mass for the whole summer.

The second trouble was more serious, because it was clear that hadn't been his first time stealing wine or wafers. Some people claimed that Riccardo and his friends were selling supposedly pre-blessed wine and bread to satanic cults from the other side of the Garigliano. Some said they gathered on the Spigno mountains too. Riccardo confessed that he got the idea of stealing from the Immacolata because you could access the cellar directly from the football pitch.

Scauri had two churches, the Immacolata and Sant'Albina, one in the square at the bottom of the hill, coming from Formia, and the other in the real main square, at the junction with the traffic lights which, like all junctions in Scauri, had the seafront on one side and the station road on the other.

Vittoria might have become one of those healers you find in little towns who apparently have no skill or purpose but live alongside nature, and not just humans. Despite everyone always asking her all sorts of things, and her real intuition for diagnosis, she had never wanted to be one. She seemed to live a quiet life, staying in the pharmacy for the hours she had to, then spending the rest of her time walking, swimming, reading botanical books, and tending the garden. She liked having people around the house, and playing cards. I'm interested in both earthly and heavenly plants, she would say, laughing.

For years, my mother and father had sought out bodily ills with a pendulum. They weren't swindlers, they were simply very religious and thought that religiosity was a flow, a sort of odourless, colourless liquid they were able to intercept, bind, and unbind.

The pendulum was black. Smooth. Possibly Bakelite. It was a strange shape, somewhere between a heart and an ice cream cone, an acorn. My daughters would play with the pendulum too, on the cat's belly, and once they used it as a strummolo, a wooden spinning top that comes back into fashion from time to time. My mother made the sign of the horns and rolled her eyes.

I wanted to go to Vittoria's house, but I didn't know what to say to Mara. I felt guilty about the holiday. If I hadn't gone to Ponza, I would probably have run into Vittoria buying pastries at Vezza's or Morelli's like every Saturday morning. We would laugh at the habit of buying pastries for Saturday lunch. Sunday is the stomach's day of rest, she would say. On Sundays, according to Franca, who went to clean the house because she was busy the other days, Vittoria stayed in the garden reading, on the patio if it was raining, under the acacia tree if it was sunny. She might stay there all afternoon, or at least that's what the Nocellas said, who had sold her the house and lived in the only other property they'd managed to hold on to, on the other side of the road. Around six in the afternoon on Sundays, Vittoria would get up and open the gate so anyone who had to leave their dog or cat would know they could come in, and usually at that point a little group of people would gather, drinking glasses of wine or beer. Mint and tamarind cordials were always on offer. Vittoria liked beer during the day, and I've seen her drink wine in the evening, not much, I don't think she got drunk. There was always something to drink at their house. Before the cat and dog boarding business in Via Romanelli, the only alcohol women came into contact with was pure or ethylated, used for cleaning windows and disinfecting scrapes and bangs on children's knees. Or to make lemon and walnut liqueurs you kept at home for occasions like weddings and funerals, and visits from relatives who lived elsewhere.

Madama spent her first stay with Mara and Vittoria under the Constantinople acacia tree. I'd never known the name of the tree until then, nor, once I knew it, could I accept the fact that a tree was named after a city, or a version of the Madonna. Some people called it sensitive mimosa, because if your fingers touched the pink flowers they would close up, and others called it a Japanese mimosa because the petals were the same colour as cherry blossom. It wasn't either of these. It wasn't even a mimosa. Over time the tree lent its name to the house, and the house, in turn, to the whole street. We'd arrange to see each other at Constantinople. In the summer, when new tourists came, this habit would cause confusion when giving directions, or when kids were arranging to meet up. The cinema's in the road parallel to Constantinople. Turn into Constantinople, it's quicker. You can't park in Constantinople after six. Things like that. It amused Vittoria, she said she liked living in Constantinople. Maybe she really was from Constantinople, for all we knew.

When Mara and Vittoria arrived, we thought they'd come out of a commune. Even in Scauri someone had tried to start one, a few years earlier, behind Monte d'Argento, but in the end the project fell through. Mostly because of the bones they found when they were digging the well. At first, everyone said they were from Roman times. But they were from the Second World War. Everyone said the commune project folded because one of the founders had recognised his grandmother's bones among the others, all mixed up like a game of Mikado.

Grandma's skull was there, he would repeat in the bar.

He'd seen his grandma's skull and it had spoken to him, that was the rumour that went around.

But was it his maternal or paternal grandma? people asked.

And what did the skull say? they insisted.

Someone suggested a petition to stop the parishes organising plays. Everyone felt like Hamlet holding a skull.

Vittoria was said to have adopted Mara. To have kidnapped her, like the children who turned up with the circus, or the cats that disappeared when the circus tent was pulled down and the cages dismantled. Many things were said, and many more were hushed up. Mara, so Germanic in colouring but so light in her movements, was said to be the daughter of Nazis who had escaped to South America, unlike Kappler and Reder, who had been imprisoned in Gaeta. It was said that Mara's parents were dead and Vittoria had taken charge of her.

However, when you saw them from the seafront, on the beach, surrounded by the dogs Mara walked, and Mara loosened her braids and danced a few steps ahead of Vittoria, turning and spinning, well, the real nature of that taking charge, of that adoption, was less clear. Her blonde hair, her hips swaying to the rhythm of some music the rest of us couldn't hear. A kidnapping. But in what sense? Vittoria dangled the arm of her glasses back and forth between her teeth.

Even the pharmacist, who held Vittoria in the highest esteem, who discussed galenic preparations with her – which had never been seen in Scauri before – as well as infusions to aid sleep or fertility, enhance moods, and facilitate the digestion of fried doughnuts from the Lido del Pino, which were very good and which you could have too many of. Even the pharmacist harboured doubts about the relationship between Vittoria and Mara. But she didn't give a damn. She was keen to stress that she was from Livorno, which had always been a free port. In short, in spite of Vittoria's cheerfulness, in spite of the intimacy we all felt with her, all we knew about her was what we saw. She was distant yet curious, welcoming yet reserved, precise yet evasive. There was a certain fatalism in the way she spoke that left you bewildered. Or fascinated. I was one of the fascinated ones. She had arrived one day with that laugh of hers that started low and finished high, she had bought a house where everyone could come in and out, she'd never argued with anyone, she'd never changed her hairstyle, and she had died in a bathtub we all knew very well while never having been in it, just because it stood at the end of the corridor, exactly opposite the front door. An accident, avvocato, a horrible accident. Bad luck.

I decided to go for a walk on the seafront before going to Vittoria's house. It was almost deserted at that time of day.

The liceo students had come out and gone home, anyone who worked was in the office, the shop, or at home doing chores, anyone who didn't was shut up in some bar, drinking and smoking. The seafront was a solitary place at three o'clock on a Tuesday in October.

So I walked and looked at the Sieci, whose furnaces hadn't been fired up for years. Luigi swore he could remember the jetties extending a way offshore to allow the cargo ships that crossed the ocean to load the bricks and transport them to South America. I used to run along them, Lea, I swear. Do me a favour, I'd answer. But I could imagine a house being rebuilt in, I don't know, Buenos Aires, and the builders down there looking at the bricks stamped with Sieci-Scauri and wondering what those names meant and where that baked and overbaked earth came from.

I looked at the sea, following the soft outline of the gulf, stared at the car park where the second-hand clothes market was held on a Wednesday. The beach clubs, each different from the last, colourful and faded in the sun. Although I was quite far away, I could hear music coming from La Bussola, a bar I tended to avoid because Luigi didn't like it. When I was level with Lido La Tintarella, I stopped, unsure whether my aversion to La Bussola proved that, despite my studies, I thought like my mother, i.e. that husbands should be heeded, without argument.

In front of the Lido Oriente I opened my diary and took out the fight photo, in which Vittoria would walk until it faded. That's what happened with Polaroid pictures. I went down onto the beach looking for the exact spot. Not that I thought I was going to find anything. Vittoria had been there on Saturday evening. Carmela had told me that Sunday morning was clear and the sea was flat and calm, but I knew that in Ponza the air had been as thick as a blanket, and this difference made me uneasy. Two points of view, two opposite impressions. The same day. I'd only accepted Alba's invitation because you could see the port from the house. Holding the photo, I identified the location of the fight and walked towards Monte d'Argento, the direction Vittoria had taken, the way to her house. When I got to Lido Maria, where the strip of sand narrows, I went over to the beach club building, which was on stilts and had both intrigued and intimidated me since I was a girl.

There were still a few canoes, a dilapidated scull, deflated rubber rings and dinghies, hard orange lifebelts from ferries, various unravelled nylon ropes. I looked into the darkness and in the darkness looking back at me there was a sudden glimmer of light. I waited for my eyes to get used to the half-light as I approached the little flash, trying not to trip. Vittoria used to wear two bracelets: one had three little bells, the other was a string of rubber or perhaps leather, fastened with two silver chain links. I think it was the bells that had made us all think of a commune. Better not to think about the two chain links at all. They looked like handcuffs, the opposite of a commune. Kneeling down to pick up the flicker of gold, I stretched out my hand, but all I found in my palm was the pearly scale of a shell.

The only two hippies in Scauri wore T-shirts and little bells. They lived, or rather camped, where Scauri turns into Marina di Minturno along the Via Appia. Here more than anywhere the houses reveal the lack of municipal and regional planning, and the surveyors' imagination has been left to run riot. Here, their creativity finds its most fertile ground and makes up for their frustration at never completing an architecture degree. Gates like spaceships or that look like enamelled Ottaviani rings, plaster ranging from lemon yellow to deep pink, houses piled up on top of one another, but not like a medieval hamlet, next to each other, a metre or two apart. In those roofless corridors between one wall and another, the windows open – not always fully – to overlook whatever the wind and bad habits carry along. Luckily, because there are many surveyors and few architects, the houses are only ever two storeys high. And this gives the town an oddly graceful appearance. The two hippies lived near Limpet, the florist, so-called because he didn't like moving around.

Manuela from the stationer's and bookshop in Piazza Rotelli told her husband, who worked in the Luccioletta bar and tended to tell everyone everything, that Vittoria had ordered a book called *I Ching*, so she might not be Catholic. The free love commune was the opposite of Catholicism, of course. This had happened at a certain time. A certain time when I had no kids and Madama was alive. However, although Vittoria and Mara didn't go to church, like more or less all of us did on a Sunday morning, each for reasons more or less similar to faith, they were always to be seen in the pews on Christmas night or Easter, and whoever happened to sit next to them swore up and down they knew the prayers, and stood up and sat down at the right times. For my part, I'd started going to church again because Giulia, at eight years old, was experiencing a moment of mystical ecstasy. I wasn't sure whether it was due to her reception year at school with the nuns or those afternoons spent with my parents, who sought out ills with the pendulum and prayed to drive them out. In any case, I had started going again to take her, and because the Communist Party, which had been my and Luigi's weekly ritual for years, no longer existed.

I gripped the pearly fragment in my hand, feeling sad, until I noticed a slight scent of tobacco and tuberose from my closed fist – the two scents that would herald Vittoria's arrival. She blended them herself. And we knew this because Grazia, who had the colonial goods shop just before Piazza Rotelli, ordered the tobacco and tuberose essential oils from Rome, which Vittoria then made into perfume. Vittoria also bought soaps there and a slender-grained rice, basmati, also fragrant. I wondered whether oil was by nature more lingering than eau de cologne, whether it was possible that I could smell it, and even whether smell is imaginary. I saw the oil stains floating on the water and Vittoria's body sinking in the black-tiled tub.

Vittoria had walked along the water's edge. Perhaps she had come over to Lido Maria, for the sculls or the windsurfing boards, which were taken somewhere else in winter but still there in October, colourful and abandoned. I had seen her sometimes, as I cycled or drove along the seafront, standing in front of the building on stilts. We all did the same things, always. We all knew everything about everyone. We all settled for what was under our noses. We all attached a certain value to form. We all knew, from habitually walking and frolicking along the esplanade, that if the tankers and cargo ships that were stationary for weeks on the horizon beyond the Gaeta promontory had been different in form, if they had been solid iron cubes, say, they would have sunk. We all knew everything about everyone. We all did the same things, always. It was easy to find each other and very easy to avoid each other.

And we're still on the difference between form and substance, I thought, reading the teachers' notes on my daughters' essays, but I kept quiet, because Luigi and I had university degrees and they didn't.

About ten years earlier, Vittoria had bought a boat. Pietro, the fisherman, had decided it was time to give it up and spend his time with his future grandchildren. He had accepted that neither of his children would become fishermen and take care of the little blue Genoese skiff that had been his longest-lasting relationship, or at least so Pietro would say. He certainly hadn't had any luck with women: he had two sons from two wives who had both died in childbirth. And his daughter-in-law would have died too, or perhaps his grandson, if Vittoria hadn't happened to be passing that way by pure chance. It was talked about in town for days, and as far as I remember, this is what happened.

Lorenzo, Pietro's elder son – who had been in my class in middle school and at the time worked in a bank, not at the counter but in the back office, since he had a degree from the University of Cassino – was at home with his wife. It might have been 1982 or 1983, it was May. When Vittoria rang the doorbell he didn't open it straight away, which he apologised for, because his wife, Sonia, was in the bathroom, she'd probably eaten a heavy dinner the night before and her stomach was upset.

Vittoria asked if she could see Sonia, who, sitting on the toilet with her skirt around her ankles, looked younger than her twenty years. Sonia apologised to Vittoria for the situation, but in such a faint voice that Vittoria took her watch off her wrist, and after a few minutes she said brusquely, perhaps authoritatively, that they needed to rush to hospital. She demanded Lorenzo's car keys and asked him to sit in the back with Sonia. She started the car, took them to the Dono Svizzero hospital in Formia, and walked back home. Nine kilometres. Near the Hotel Europa, Tommaso – Luigi's friend, who was already hanging around the hospital but wasn't yet a medical examiner – stopped to offer her a lift, but Vittoria thanked him curtly, saying that she'd rather walk home, and that Lorenzo was arrogant and that men, males, are dangerous. The stupider they are, the worse it is, for goodness' sake, she said. Tommaso told Luigi, who told me. And I remember it well. I'd never liked Lorenzo.

This intervention of Vittoria's had been providential because there had indeed been an issue of faeces, but not the mother's. The baby had passed meconium and, although he was later born perfectly healthy, he was poisoning himself in her womb.

The whole story, from delivering the woman in labour to the nurses, to her return on foot, the timely diagnosis, and Sonia's very, very faint voice as she sat on the toilet, was recounted by one of the midwives to Tommaso, who worked in the hospital. The midwife was close to retirement, and haloed with the sanctity of knowing how to deliver breech babies without having to resort to a Caesarean, using "the manoeuvre", as she called it, accompanying the word with a gesture, an anticlockwise rotation, the same gesture that denotes mixing or covert scheming. Anyway, this midwife assured him she had never heard anyone talk like Vittoria, not even a doctor, a ward manager, never mind an assistant pharmacist, basically a shop assistant. And from Scauri, too. But you've no idea, the midwife remarked, in amazement, how accurately she told this and that person, and even me, what to do.

In town, we wondered for days whether someone from Formia had ever complimented someone from Scauri before, and no, they never had. I think that was when Vittoria became Scaurese. And she hadn't even been in Scauri that long. I think that was when we realised there was something special about Vittoria. Sonia later confessed that while Vittoria's tone had upset her, her presence had comforted her, and she had even thought Vittoria was kind of sexy.

So when Pietro decided to sell his boat, he asked Vittoria, not because he thought she'd be interested but because he trusted her advice. He was sure that with all her dealings with the pharmacy and the pet boarding business, she would know someone who'd be interested in the boat. Vittoria asked the price and told Pietro she'd take it, provided he guaranteed her the space in the dock and also sold her the trailer to transport it. She would keep it in the garden, behind the house, during the winter. Perhaps Pietro could help her build a carport for it.

And so Vittoria was the first woman to own a boat space at the dock, an exclusively male club. Every year the film *Around the World in 80 Days* would be on TV, with David Niven as Phileas Fogg, the man who has bet all his money and has to complete a trip around the world and return, by a specific day and time, to London, to the Reform Club, an exclusive men-only club where he is a member. And he manages it, but he brings a woman with him, the Indian princess he has fallen in love with. After Vittoria bought the boat, the dock started to seem like the Reform Club with neon lights, and Vittoria's face had a hint of something Indian and, at heart, regal.

No one had thought Vittoria capable of sailing a boat until then. Pietro, who had insisted on accompanying her, despite her protests, on a first trip towards Gaeta, later told the whole of Bar Italia that he didn't know a woman could perform certain manoeuvres and tie certain knots.

The carport was built and, over the years, strange rows of violets, broom, and pinkish-white bellflowers grew up over the scaffolding pipes and corrugated sheeting, lusher and more lasting than the ones that twisted around canes near ditches, or at the Capo d'Acqua stream, or climbed up walls, their leaves like the decorations on the Corinthian capitals in the church of the old port at Gaeta. Vittoria also had a bed of nettles. For cooking, she said. I got stung on my calves. And I wasn't the only one.

Vittoria had died in her bathtub and I couldn't believe it. Vittoria, who had cured us, or not, with her herbal concoctions, and enabled the birth of a baby who would otherwise have been stillborn. Who had bought a house and a boat. Who lived with a woman who could have been her daughter. Who tried to have an answer for everyone, which made us believe she might have an answer for everything, and in so doing comforted us. Vittoria had died and I couldn't understand why. But I was sure there was a reason. I needed the reason for Vittoria's death.

Sonia had insisted on naming her son Vittorio, and Lorenzo couldn't oppose it, nor could Pietro, although he had hoped the first grandchild would be named after him. But Sonia was resolute, also because, before handing her over to the nurses pushing the stretcher, Vittoria had given her a bottle containing some unknown liquid which had soothed the pain of the emergency Caesarean they had been forced to perform practically in the hospital corridor. When she bought the boat, Vittoria assured Pietro that if his grandson grew up to love the sea she would leave it to him, Mara wasn't interested in boats anyway and could barely swim. Which had caused the town to reconsider the nature of the relationship between Mara and Vittoria: if she was talking about inheritance, things to be left, there must be some blood relationship. Perhaps Mara was living with her aunt. I think it was the buying and selling of the boat that caused the matter of the house in Via Romanelli to resurface. Its deeds, which had been drawn up about ten years previously, were in Mara's name. The notary involved had died in the meantime, and no one in Bar Italia could remember the exact wording. By now the house was essentially Constantinople, which has been there in myth since the beginning of time.

Constantinople is one of the streets joining the Via Appia to Via Olivella, which runs along the railway. Scauri has three parallel streets, Luigi says, measuring the distance from the beach to the countryside. The seafront, the Via Appia, and Via Olivella. The other streets run lengthwise between them, including Constantinople. It's an elegant street, if that adjective means anything when applied to Scauri. For a while there was a photocopy shop opposite Vittoria and Mara's house, then the local Communist Party headquarters, and now there was a vehicle documentation centre I'd never seen anyone enter. It was a street of slightly better-off, professional people. An ear, nose, and throat specialist lived there, a maths teacher, an English teacher, a Polish playwright and poet for six months of the year, and a couple of grain merchants, and the Nocellas, who lived above the vehicle office. Holidaymakers rented the other houses in the street in summer. The houses must have been expensive: they were set well apart and surrounded by some greenery, if not gardens. It was the only street still holding out against anodised aluminium shutters and sun awnings. The shop that sold them prospered on the Via Appia, a short way away.

When Luigi and I had renovated our house the year before, we had given in to anodised aluminium. We'd preferred to spend the money we had on another bathroom rather than restoring wooden shutters.

With the little bell in my head and the shell in my pocket, I set off towards Vittoria's house, certain that sooner or later I'd have to convince myself that the accident in the bathtub had happened, no matter how much of the past I unravelled trying to deceive myself she was still alive. Gradually no one would talk about Vittoria any more, even I would stop thinking about her. I was sorry the weekend in Ponza had prevented me from saying goodbye one last time. I resented Alba for inviting me. And myself for accepting.

There were a dozen or so people at the house, the usual faces. The Nocellas, the pharmacist with her three daughters, Filomena, Pietro the fisherman, Sonia and Vittorio, still in short trousers, Councillor Comi and his wife, the railwaymen from the club. Mara was preparing something like punch in what looked like a goldfish bowl, and chanting to herself over and over, Kir royale is Vittoria's favourite, but we've almost run out of cassis. Cassis was another product no one in Scauri had ever heard of before Vittoria came, and thanks to – or because of – Vittoria they had started buying it. They even had it at the Bar Haiti, by the traffic lights on Via Olivella, and the bar at the railwaymen's club opposite the station, places where Vittoria used to go and play cards. She was a great one for playing cards.

I went over to Mara and, not knowing what to say, hugged her. Mara held me tight and I thought she would never let me go, but almost immediately she pulled away, saying I have to feed the snake.

That's how I realised, with Vittoria's body in the other room, that exotic animals also live among us, and not only in houses in glossy magazines. I looked at the sofa, nice but a bit worn, the Thonet chairs with stiff, old Vienna straw seats which would soon crack. The rugs with bald spots here and there, the beautiful unmatched plates and glasses, an Arabian-looking silver teapot. The house smelt of lavender and of Vittoria, her oils, despite the dogs and cats who were habitual guests and long-term tenants.

The bedroom was simple: a very narrow, dark wood double bed that looked like a boat with a mattress inside, a long, low, powder-blue dresser, darkened with the years, beautiful white linen sheets with a lace trim my mother would have envied out loud – was it tatting lace? I'd never learned to knit or crochet – plus two stools instead of bedside tables, dark like the bed and with legs that echoed its curves, a sliding door with a glimpse of dresses, hanging beyond, and a chest of drawers. Snakes and walk-in wardrobes. In Scauri.

Vittoria was lying on the bed, her arms by her sides, dressed in her white linen trousers, with a pair of black espadrilles that looked new, judging by the soles, and an ocean-blue cotton shirt with three-quarter-length sleeves. Summer clothes. She liked the texture of linen, I remembered that. Anyway, the dead don't feel the cold. She didn't look like she was sleeping, and despite the make-up a bluish-yellow tone was emerging on the skin of her face and hands, like the colour of that dresser and that faded, light sleeveless dress I had seen her wearing so many times. Mara had left just one of the two rings she used to wear on her finger, and the other was lying on the bedside stool. She was wearing her bracelets. I bent over and counted the little bells. I took the piece of shell from my pocket and put it in hers. When Mara came to call me, she found me with my hands on Vittoria's wrist.

I'm so sorry, Mara.

She was such a good swimmer. If she was alive she'd be enjoying this, preposterous stories made her laugh, she enjoyed funerals. Dying like this, it's like a joke, it would have cheered her up.

You think?

Of course. She used to say the funniest phrase in the world was There is infinite hope, but not for us. I don't know if she made it up, though, or read it somewhere.

Mara started laughing, took my hand, and dragged me into the living room, where everyone was talking about Vittoria and drinking Kir to her memory, the same gestures with which we had toasted her good health. I drank too.

I asked Mara if she had noticed any change, if Vittoria had confided that she felt ill or tired. No, Mara said, she was more cheerful than usual on Saturday. In fact, she said, lowering her voice, we had a few drinks and then we did it. It hadn't happened for ages, I thought she didn't fancy me any more. It did seem odd to me that she didn't go out to play cards like every Saturday, but then we started drinking and all the rest, and I didn't think about it, and when I woke up in the morning to walk the dogs, she'd already gone out.

Mara's breath smelt of alcohol.

I blushed and Mara leaned in to kiss me on the cheek, she was wearing Vittoria's perfume and smiling. She was beautiful.

At home, I told Luigi about the Kir, the snake, and the walk-in wardrobe, the evening Vittoria and Mara had shared, the sentence about hope which Luigi didn't find funny. I still wasn't sure if it made me laugh, but more yes than no.

Luigi said he'd heard at the railwaymen's club, where he'd stopped off on his way back from Naples, that the pensioners there had been the first to worry about Vittoria because she hadn't turned up to play cards on Saturday night. On Sunday morning, Franca, who had to go to their house anyway, had gone half an hour early because her husband Salvatore had asked What's happened to Vittoria, she hasn't missed a game of briscola in twenty years.

Luigi came over and kissed me on the lips, sliding a hand down almost under my buttocks, and I pushed my hips against his. I knew Luigi still fancied me and that I fancied him, a lot. Silvia came in, yelling that her sister Giulia had broken one of her dolls, and started crying. Luigi said I'll go, and I stayed in the kitchen, watching the convection motions in the water heating on the stove. I'd rediscovered them the week before, testing Silvia on science.

That night I had a dream. In it, I was still living at home with my parents. I received a letter from the police station in Latina. I opened it. I read the letter inside, which said I couldn't apply to be a police inspector because I was too short. I ripped up the envelope and crumpled the letter into a ball. Someone rang the doorbell and I hurried to open it, annoyed. Vittoria was standing there in an inspector's uniform, looking at me with those liquid eyes of hers, the arm of her glasses in her mouth, and I looked away. Vittoria was at least ten centimetres shorter than me.

I got up early with the idea of going to the office before the funeral. I didn't want to take the photograph of the fight and other documents with me and risk losing them. A black Mercedes was parked outside the front, a very new one given the numbers following ROMA on the number plate. As I inserted my key in the lock, the rear door of the car opened sharply and an elegant older man looked out from the back seat, tall and lanky with pale-green eyes, age spots on the backs of his hands and dark nicotine stains on the inside of his right index and middle fingers. He was wearing a black trench coat and a light, brimmed Borsalino hat. Everything he was wearing was black, except his shirt. When he tipped the brim of his hat I was sure he wasn't about to ask for some information.

I am Giorgio Pontecorvo d'Aquino. I'm defending young Antonello Antonelli, he said. His parents are both dear friends of my nephews. I couldn't come and see you earlier, avvocato, and I'm here on other business. I was wondering whether you have time for an interview this afternoon. I think we should settle to avoid court. My clients and young Antonello would like to reach an agreement and obviously a financial settlement. I'm sure we both want to avoid sullying two such young men with criminal records, no one was trying to kill anyone else, these things happen. I believe I was guilty of similar silliness myself at their age, but it's been so very long that it may be wishful thinking rather than a memory.

He stretched his lips into a smile. He must have been a handsome man once. Now he was more elegant than handsome.

Certainly, avvocato, we could meet at four or five, as you like.

I'd prefer five. I have an appointment before that and cannot estimate how long it will take.

Let's say five then.

Avvocato Russo.

Yes?

Are there many steps up to your office?

Forty-eight.

Then would you mind if we moved our little talk elsewhere?

Of course not.

You tell me, I don't know the town.

We can meet at five at Lo Scoglio.

Thank you.

Avvocato Pontecorvo.

Yes?

Why do you mention two criminal records? It was your client who threw the bottle and broke my client's nose.

But it was your client who misinterpreted high spirits as malicious intent, punched mine, and came off worst.

There are no trials of intent, there are only facts, and I stick to those. Also, Avvocato Pontecorvo, there is a photo of your client throwing the bottle, a Polaroid, the boy is taking aim.

I'll see you at five o'clock, it's going to be a very pleasant chat. Thank you, signora.

Not at all, thank you, signore.

He got back in the car, touching the brim of his hat with that gesture already as grim as it was familiar. He sat in the back. The driver, whose features I couldn't make out, started the engine. Leaving the photo on my desk, I looked once more at the figure of Vittoria in the background and realised I'd never known her surname before reading the death notices. The black-edged ones I looked out for wherever I went, as if the dead always know something about the living. Vittoria Basile. She was born in Rome. She'd just turned sixty-four. Luigi would have known if she'd had a birthday party without my realising. But she hadn't celebrated.

The square in front of the church was packed, for the second time in a few short years. On 30 January 1989 Gisella Treglia was killed, her body found in the pinewoods, burnt, with one leg broken at the knee. Gisella was seventeen and studying to be a nursery school teacher. She had last been seen at the newsagent's opposite the bar. She was said to have been talking to a tall, dark-haired girl of her own age whom no one knew or recognised and who could not be traced over the course of the following days. We would all come to doubt her existence. The investigation lasted about ten days. The carabinieri of Scauri, Sessa Aurunca, and Formia interviewed hundreds of people, fifty-six in the first two days, and a wave of fear spread as quickly as a rumour – this was a serial killer's first murder. In mid February, the Formia police arrested nineteen-year-old Alfonso Coppola, who had gone to Gisella asking her to act as a go-between between him and his ex-girlfriend, Gisella's cousin. He had killed her, he confessed to the carabinieri. When Gisella had accused him of violence towards her cousin, he had lost his temper and punched her. Thinking he had killed her, he had taken her into the pinewoods, stabbed her body seventeen times, and burned it, to simulate a satanic ritual.

Vittoria had come to see me in the office, upset by this murder. If the boy had been able to see Gisella wasn't dead, she said, he might not have killed her. Vittoria talked for a long time, her face turned to the window. She usually preferred smiles to words, but that time she hadn't smiled once. She had stressed the violence of human beings. Systemic, not casual. I wondered if by human beings she meant men, males, or whether these human beings included me, or her. I wondered whether she herself might have been subjected to that same violence, but I kept quiet. I wondered whether she had stabbed anyone. I hadn't, yet.

It's love that is terrible, I said to her, when at last she stopped looking out of the window.

Love's got nothing to do with things like this, Lea, it's the sense of ownership, occupation of territory. We all know it, it starts in the family. I'm not saying families necessarily create monsters. I'm saying that because we've lived in families, we all know that feelings of guilt come from the thought that one has a life outside it, whatever life it may be. I'm not talking about affairs, just a job, an interest. The prospect of a diploma or a degree.

And does that happen to everyone?

Men put up with less than women, but it annoys everyone, male or female. Men, though, are used to possessing, controlling, history is on their side, and they're less inclined to put up with the existence of a life outside the family, their family. Think about this boy, Lea, this killer, he didn't even have a family life with Gisella's cousin, but he couldn't stand that Gisella, his girlfriend's cousin, did. And it was a life he wasn't involved in. She wanted to be a teacher.

I was scared for Silvia, who, at ten years old, was starting to go around Scauri on her own, and even more afraid to present the world to her as a hostile place.

I'm scared, I told Vittoria.

We fail, but we mustn't think it's impossible to protect the people we love, that's why we mustn't love too many, it's tiring protecting them. Sometimes we might even win, added Vittoria triumphantly, smiling at last. Don't make that face, Lea, we're not made to suffer, sometimes we give in to suffering, but we mustn't make a habit of it. Don't be afraid for your girls, don't think about love, don't be sentimental, so many romantic notions. Forget that, talk to Gisella's parents, give them support. It'll be all the more welcome because you know the law and how it works.

Perhaps Father Michele would be better, or a psychologist.

Not you too with the psychologists, Lea? There's no such thing as the inner life, it's just an excuse to behave badly.

If it happened to Silvia or Giulia, I replied, I wouldn't wait for any law, any justice, any lawyer, I'd act off my own bat.

I suppose that's what motherhood does, she whispered.

I don't trust justice, Vittoria, what use is justice? If everything happened according to good sense, respect, the ability to keep one's word, we wouldn't need the law, it's a place where the truth is worth nothing any more.

But where is the truth worth anything, Lea? Don't you see how romantic your ideas are? Anyway, I'll go now, at your age I had a lot to do and I didn't like interruptions.

It's possible to win, Vittoria repeated, standing up and smiling again in that melancholic yet cheerful way of hers. Levantine. Shy and grave. Timid and bold.

One last thing, Lea, precisely because we aren't made to suffer, you're right, we surround ourselves with a lot of useless things in order to live, so as we move on we have the chance to lighten our load, take up less space, in the hope that whoever comes after us will find their own and do better.

I wondered when I had said this thing that Vittoria had understood, and if any of the words either of us had said concerned her. Vittoria, whose clothes were as unfussy as her speech, who dug a hole for fruit and vegetable scraps in her garden behind the house where she kept the boat in winter and separated paper from plastic and glass from metal long before separating rubbish became a practice, and didn't have a single piece of waxed paper, Tupperware container, or roll of cling film in her home. Who didn't have pierced ears. Who could stay at the beach alone for half a day at a time, without speaking to anyone. How much did those words about useless things concern her? While I continued asking myself questions I would never know the answer to, Vittoria opened the door again, without knocking.

Take these drops, Lea, no more than ten a day, herbal, they'll calm you down.

But I.

Like every small-town funeral, there were curious onlookers. Because the square and therefore the church are directly accessible from the Via Appia, they usually take advantage of the traffic lights or the junction to slow down and take a look. So when I saw Avvocato Pontecorvo's car pull over with its hazard lights on and another two cars, another Mercedes and a BMW – a Three Letters, as we called them from Scauri all the way down the rest of Campania – I didn't immediately realise they were there for Vittoria's funeral.

But they were.

They got out of the cars: the lawyer, a younger woman with a man who was holding her arm, and two lads, perhaps twins, aged no more than twenty, and a woman of about fifty with a blonde boy about sixteen years of age whose face was familiar to me. They were all very elegant, very formal, and they all walked down the central aisle, straight ahead. Only the teenager turned towards Mara and bowed his head in greeting. As I followed them, I realised that Mara and all the rest of us were sitting in the pews on the right, while these strangers were on the left, occupying only the first two pews. No one sat behind them. If the church had been a ferry for Ponza, and we were the cars, it would have been unbalanced.

Father Michele talked about Vittoria, how she was devoted to the community, the foraging excursions she organised with the boys and girls of the primary school, and the herbarium each child compiled, the anatomy workshops, and the hours of French and English conversation she offered those confronted with a language they'd never heard.

Questions occurred to me that I'd never thought to ask before.

Where had Vittoria learned languages, anatomy, botany? The commune we'd all imagined might be international, of course. The peacock, which had turned up at a certain point, was a gift from Vittoria to Mara. The peacock transforms poison into another substance. The peacock is a symbol of longevity. Patrick, the peacock, lived in Via Romanelli, Scauri, in a house inhabited by two women who could have been mother and daughter and were not. A peacock in Constantinople.

I met a girl at university who was the daughter of a literature professor of Argentinian origin, from Buenos Aires. He had met the girl's mother while she was living in a women-only commune in Holland. I hadn't asked myself as many questions about the international nature of the commune as I had about the other issue. Women only. Women who went with men, like my friend's mother, or women who went with each other?

Peacocks, communes, herbs, *I Ching*, tamarind cordial, basmati rice. Men put up with less than women, Lea.

Instead, the shiny, expensive cars, the overcoats and brogues or other formal shoes, the hats and gloves, didn't point to a commune, international or otherwise, women-only or otherwise, but to solid wealth that would explain a few things about Vittoria's life – like the purchase of a house in an almost elegant street, the precious unmatched plates, the knowledge of languages – but not others, not everything. Living in Scauri, for example. Gathering scraps of conversation between one prayer and another, I realised that those faces weren't new only to me. The others and I watched the pharmacist, anxious to catch the flicker of an eyebrow. But she remained upright and Junoesque, her eyes on the altar, her hair piled up like a monument thanks to Cielo Alto hairspray. It was a while before I identified the irregular, frenetic clicking, which seemed at first to come from outside. It was her fingers tapping the back of the prie-dieu.

It was beyond my powers of imagination to try and guess or understand, on the spur of the moment, what Avvocato Pontecorvo was doing there. After all, until a short while ago I hadn't even known Vittoria Basile's surname.

*

At the end of Mass, Father Michele sent for me via an altar boy, Luca, the younger son of Tatiana from the grocer's. Luca attended church with my youngest, Giulia, and he wasn't very well behaved. But despite my enormous empathy for my daughter, it was hard for me to show antipathy towards the boy, so I ruffled his hair to remind myself that one mustn't harm growing flesh.

Although he must have been used to hiding his reactions, Avvocato Pontecorvo gave a start, skilfully masked by a cough, when I entered the rectory. I was astonished to find him there as well. He stood up.

Avvocato Russo, he addressed me. I've only been here a few hours and it's already clear to me that not so much as a leaf moves in this little town without you.

His knuckles, gripping the handle of his stick, were white with effort.

I looked at him, annoyed, not by his unctuous compliment but by the diminutive applied to Scauri, the place where I was born, where I had continued to live, and which functioned like a concertina, its six thousand residents in winter months expanding to almost a hundred thousand in summer. Father Michele invited me to sit. He was sweating but looked pleased. No longer subdued. Perhaps priests are like doctors – after a while death and its ritual become habitual, and habits are comforting.

Lea, Avvocato Pontecorvo is Vittoria's husband, they were married in London in 1954 and they never divorced. He would like to take the remains to the family vault in Verano cemetery. I've already told him Vittoria bought two plots in the cemetery here, in the ground, because she wanted to be buried, not in the niches, and she hated family vaults. Do you remember when she criticised the demolition of the old columbaria to make room for vaults with aluminium gates? They looked like terraced houses. But with dead people inside. Apartments for the dead, Vittoria called them. Remember how she laughed?

Father Michele went on talking to Avvocato Pontecorvo about extending the cemetery, and repeating demographical matters relating to parish registers, making jokes about undertakers, and recounting vague ghost stories. I thought about Vittoria, and what would happen to her jumpers. I would like to have one. Would the bars stop ordering crème de cassis for Kir, or had we got used to it now?

Avvocato Pontecorvo managed to interrupt Father Michele's embarrassed rambling.

Father, I think my colleague will agree that I can take my wife's body back home.

I wondered if the word *home* meant the same to Avvocato Pontecorvo as it did to me. I reminded myself that they had never divorced.

The church of Sant'Albina was a reinforced-concrete monstrosity designed and built by someone who must have studied Le Corbusier without understanding him. Or perhaps I didn't understand him. That might be true. I had grown up in a town where architects were considered pretentious, and where two girls in Giulia's class were called

Enea, a boy's name, because it ended in "a". I could accept that I might not understand the architecture of a mouse-grey reinforced-concrete church with a polygonal floor plan, out of whose slits – not windows – the branches of pine trees were visible. After all, Vittoria was suddenly dead. And suddenly married. I'd never known that in twenty years either.

I started talking, addressing the pine cones balanced on the branches, green beyond the glass.

Avvocato Pontecorvo, it would be both a mistake and painful to end up in court over a matter like this. Above all, there is no room for judgement.

I am within my rights.

That's not the case, Avvocato Pontecorvo. The purchase of the plot and the payment made to Paradiso funeral directors are a clear indication of intention.

Your undertakers are called Paradiso?

It's a surname, Avvocato Pontecorvo.

So in Scauri you all die and go to Paradiso? And do you stay there forever?

I understand the irony, but that is the case, yes.

Help me to understand, Avvocato Russo. Did Vittoria buy two plots in Paradiso in order to bury her top half in one and her bottom half in the other? Did she pay for two funerals? I knew my wife well, she was vainglorious, but she was not that type. From the waist down and from the waist up?

One of the plots is in the name of Mara Amadasi.

I am not aware of any family relationship with Signora Amadasi, but it wouldn't surprise me at all if Vittoria had gifted a cemetery plot, she's always been a rather original woman.

Mara and Vittoria lived together.

I don't believe co-tenants can claim rights to the dead, but perhaps I am overlooking some laws or regulations that you are more familiar with. Or is it something that concerns the burial of emperors, Avvocato Russo, do you think? One is buried with all one's property, things, and people.

I prefer to think there is a usucapion for things, that they can be transferred to cohabitants.

Father, your parishioner wants to set a precedent!

No, Avvocato Pontecorvo, I don't want to set a precedent, I answered, resisting the temptation to hold up a hand in front of Father Michele's mouth, which was about to open. Addressing the pine cones once again, I repeated, I don't want to set a precedent, but I would like to see the wishes respected of a person who has participated in community life and who was integrated in the town. And I would like this to be done out of love. However, should love not be enough, because it hardly ever is, there are the law courts. May I remind you that death dissolves all ties, even matrimonial ones. The dead, Avvocato Pontecorvo, belong to no one.

All at once Pontecorvo, who in my eyes now seemed little more than a well-dressed older gentleman, stood up, took his leave of Father Michele with a little bow, and said to me We have an appointment at your office at five o'clock, we shall discuss this as well, I hope you will reflect in the meantime.

Then, just outside the door, allowing us to admire his authoritative and aquiline three-quarter profile, still sharp if thickened with the years, he coughed and, like a consummate actor, whispered a final phrase.

I suppose, my dear sir and madam, you know the nature of the relationship between the woman who made me a widower today and Mara Amadasi.

Without waiting for a reaction or response, he set off, jamming his hat on his head, and did not look back. The tapping of his stick on the marble was irregular.

Why does he have to come to your office, Lea?

Not the office, we're meeting at Lo Scoglio.

Oh Lord, why didn't you tell him?

He's the lawyer representing the boy from Rome who broke the ironmonger's son's nose last Saturday.

Ah, the lad needs to watch himself.

But he didn't start it.

It doesn't matter who starts it, Lea, fighting is wrong.

Father Michele took an envelope from the drawer, one of the ones with a plastic window. I should have remembered to tell Cristina that there were only two left in the office, she should have gone to Registri Buffetti to buy some. The envelope was sealed with wax, and a handwritten lined sheet was visible through the window.

What's that?

Vittoria's will.

Why didn't you give it to her husband, who is also a lawyer?

Because Vittoria told me that if anything unexpected happened, I was to give it to you, and since we're here, I'll give you mine too.

What are you saying, Father Miche'?

I'm saying that I'm the same age as Vittoria and if I fall asleep in the bath I don't want anyone burying me at Prima Porta. Have you ever been to Prima Porta, Lea?

Just once, when Aunty Gina died. You remember Grandma's sister, the one who was married in Rome?

Gina, yes, what a lovely person she was. Verano would have been better, but there isn't an iota of space. Who knows who Vittoria will be put with. Here she has her two metres of earth, she wanted herbs on top, she said that way anyone passing could take home a sprig of rosemary or sage or thyme, and marjoram, lemongrass, and lemon balm, she even wanted garlic, imagine.

Why didn't Vittoria give me her will herself?

She didn't think she was going to die. Heavens, how young you are. Out of superstition.

I turned to the pine cones on the branches again. I'd never thought Vittoria superstitious, and I still didn't. But why then, if death is the one certainty, did Father Michele say *unexpected*? Or had Vittoria used that word herself?

Catholicism is not entirely certain about mothers. The father, for example, was more certain about Jesus.

I didn't think I was young. I hadn't thought so since I first gave birth.

Saying goodbye to Father Michele, I slipped the will into

my bag. Vittoria wasn't a superstitious person, and she isn't now, I said clearly in my head, while I followed in Avvocato Pontecorvo's footsteps.

I suppose you know the nature of the relationship between the woman who made me a widower today and Mara Amadasi. Vittoria wanted thyme on her grave.

I thought of Sonia again, how when she told the story of the birth she and her child managed to survive, she never failed to mention that Vittoria was kind of sexy. I thought of Vittoria, too, when I'd met her one day coming back from the cliffs, her hair still wet, tied back, and seeing me driving past she stuck out her thumb, like a hitch-hiker. Vittoria was playful. I stopped and said to her, also playfully, Where are you going, lovely lady? I'll go anywhere you want to take me, lovely lady, she replied. But we've met before, haven't we? I insisted. Yes, we've met, replied Vittoria, leaning against the window. I don't remember where, I went on, stretching to open the door and putting my face very close to hers. Nor do I, said Vittoria, pulling the door, nor do I, she repeated, getting in and patting me on the thigh, but I remember you.

The pharmacist was waiting for me outside, sitting on a bench, smoking. Around her, some children were chasing after a deflated Super Santos ball. Mara was there too, looking at the ground, sweeping the pine needles into little huts with the toe of her shoe. I checked my watch, I wanted to stop off at home, take a shower and change for my meeting with Pontecorvo, and I wanted to cuddle my daughters. Mara stayed where she was, without raising her head or stopping her demolition of the pine needle village, but the pharmacist came towards me. I pre-empted her.

I'm sorry, Lina, but I have to go, I want to stop off at home before my afternoon appointments.

Lea, did you know she was married to that lawyer?

I clutched the strap of my bag. How come the town always knew everything about everyone before everyone else?

No, I didn't, Father Michele told me just now. The husband wants to take Vittoria back to Rome.

And he can only take her back now she's dead, Lea. If Vittoria wanted to go back to Rome, she'd have already gone. She wanted to stay here instead, she chose to stay here, she didn't like going to Rome.

Did she go often?

A couple of times a year, perhaps three, I'd have to check. More lately. As you can imagine, Vittoria was very meticulous, she noted down everything in the pharmacy register.

You have a register?

The register's actually for the medicines we give out, but when she came to the pharmacy she started using it like an attendance register. She said that it was better to know who had been on the counter in case of mistakes, it made it easier to act and avoid the worst, you know what she was like.

And why did she go to Rome?

What, you never go to Rome?

Mara joined us, she hugged me and started crying. I stroked her hair like I would with my girls, even though Mara and I were almost the same age. Lina looked at me a bit suspiciously. I went on stroking Mara's head, unable to comfort her. I could feel the dampness of her tears through my blouse. Then, still crying, she let go of my shoulders and thanked me.

Mara, did you know she was married?

Of course I did, Lea, that's how I met her, because she was married, but I must say I'd forgotten after so many years. I never thought I'd see that lawyer again. I swear, Vittoria had no intention of spending eternity in the family vault.

He has no right, Mara, but I understand him trying, she's his wife. *Was* his wife.

But how do you spend eternity anyway, Le', if eternity is what it is?

Lina rolled her eyes, and after that ridiculous question Mara did something ridiculous. She started screaming, fists clenched, feet stamping the ground. Whether it was pain or madness I don't know, but the sound was a dull whimpering of grinding teeth. A crushing of bones. She sniffed and stared at me, angrily.

I slept in the same bed with Vittoria every night for the last twenty years, don't come telling me that she was married to that man, because it's unfair and it's wrong under the laws of men and under God's law, or anybody's law you want. Anyway, in your job God's truth doesn't exist, nor does the truth of hands, the only truth that exists is the trial, right, Le'?

Exhausted, Mara collapsed to the ground, in the middle of the square, and everything stopped as if it had been switched off, except the ball, which continued to bounce insolently in our direction, kicked by a little girl and helped on its way by a boy who was fixated on an adult woman falling to the ground as if in a belated, solitary ring o' roses. The two children were too different in age to my daughters for me to know them. The ball bounced on Mara's back, and she grasped it violently, raised it to her mouth, and bit into it. The deflated ball muffled her screams, the sound was like the foaming of waves on the pebbles at Sassolini beach. I'll burst it for you! Mara screamed in the direction of the children when she hurled it at them, covered in spit. Lina the pharmacist lit another cigarette. All right, she said, let's go and eat something now, perhaps our blood sugar's a bit low. Lina was an imposing woman and she, too, had had a different type of life from ours. We called her Big Lina behind her back, and sometimes to her face. And sometimes she referred to herself that way, in the third person. Not today, though.

Mara calmed down at home. Vito the long-haired ginger cat came over to her, very affectionately, while the dog, Sibilla, a cross between a wolfdog and a dachshund, stayed there where Vittoria always sat, and without moving she raised her ears and then lowered them again.

Thanks for walking me home.

It was on my way.

It seems stupid to say this now, Lea, but I've been jealous of you so many times. I'm sorry about what I said in the square, I know you're a good lawyer, everyone says so, and everyone comes to you, Vittoria came too, didn't she?

Jealous?

Yes, because Vittoria enjoyed talking to you.

How do you mean?

School, those sorts of things, culture. What's culture anyway?

I don't know what to tell you.

You don't have to tell me anything, I just wanted to thank you for walking me home and tell you I was jealous of you.

But I didn't like Vittoria in that way.

The way you like something doesn't matter, it matters that you like it, and in the end, when you like it and get close enough to it you end up inside it.

On the patio a black cat with a sprinkling of white on its chest was scratching the wooden planks. Digging, almost as if there was something underneath. Or someone. What do cats see? Don't worry, Mara said, keeping her eyes on a glass left on the table which must have contained alcohol. Take no notice, he must be trying to catch a lizard. He doesn't kill them, their tails come off.

I didn't know you had another cat.

It's Gallina Nera, he belongs to Gino from the railwaymen's club. He's been here for three days, since Vittoria went. She and Gino were good friends, and maybe the cat.

What?

Nothing, the cat kills birds.

I don't remember where, I don't remember where we've met before, lovely lady, but I remember you. The way you like someone doesn't matter, Lea, the point is that when you get close to people you end up inside. What do cats see. Nothing, the cat kills birds.

I left, with a last glance at the bathroom with its black tiles and irregular coloured panes. I thought about Vittoria, lying in the bath, lit up by green, pink, yellow light, colours I'd never seen her wear. Or at least I didn't think I had. The ginger cat was asleep in the middle of the table, indifferent. Walking home, I answered absent-mindedly when someone occasionally asked why I was out and about at that time. The town is the place where everyone knows everything about everyone. The hatred I'd felt for Scauri as a girl was back. A feeling of airlessness. I felt imprisoned. I'd learned to play chess well at sixteen, seventeen years old, because there are only two things you can do in prison, learn to read or play chess. Or you can flip a coin and note down when it's heads or tails. Or at least so I'd read in a volume of *Reader's Digest*. On the opposite page was an advert for detergent. And through chess I'd met and fallen in love with Luigi. Perhaps we both fell in love. Even though he was already at university and could get out of prison with a second-class season ticket, Scauri-Minturno to Naples. Luigi said no, he was one of the ones who had to go back to his cell at night. Luigi was a keen communist. His father and mother weren't at all; on the contrary, his dad had volunteered for the war in Africa and stayed there twelve years, he'd been a staunch fascist. I loved my father-in-law, the fascist alpine trooper, very much, despite having caught him several times singing my daughters to sleep with "Faccetta Nera", with his fluting voice that faded away gradually as the girls yielded to the charm of his aquamarine eyes. Luigi had his father's green eyes, streaked with the grey of his mother's. In the end we stayed living in Scauri, Luigi didn't like anywhere else, and I complied. We furnished the prison, we had two daughters in prison. Perhaps they would manage to escape. I wanted them to study, travel, learn languages. If I'd been sixteen now perhaps I would have broken noses and thrown bottles on the beach. I'd have stolen communion wafers and wine like Riccardo.

And yet Vittoria had chosen to live in Scauri.

Luigi hated private property. He also hated paying rent. So we lived in a house that belonged to his parents. As guests, but pure, light ones. This is what he must have thought, without saying so, and perhaps without even knowing. And he was lazy. But I couldn't even move a piece of furniture. I didn't have the whole prison at my disposal, just one cell.

I'd never liked Vittoria in that way. Sonia never forgot to stress that Vittoria had been kind of sexy that day. I didn't know whether Vittoria had known that most of us were under her spell, or whether she didn't care, it didn't matter to her, and therefore she wasn't surprised and took no notice.

Compliments should never be asked for, rejected, or repeated, she would tell the children who boasted about their herbaria. And the parents who boasted about their children.

At home, Silvia and Giulia were eating. They had a longer school day on Wednesdays and they had lunch late. Paola, the woman who had been picking them up and spending part of the afternoon with them for a few months, had cooked them boiled green beans and a slice of meat. All three of them were sitting at the table, eating, and watching Wanna Marchi selling beauty products. I had cheered up before I even opened the door and went to sit down.

Would you like me to cook you something? asked Paola in her mellow Naples hinterland accent. I shook my head, still contemplating the devoted attention with which the girls watched the shopping channel. I realised that Paola and Wanna Marchi looked alike. If Paola had red hair, she'd be Wanna Marchi.

Locked in the bathroom, I lit a cigarette and turned on the water to run a bath.

Not even a coffee, Lea? yelled Paola and I answered No, without much conviction and without raising my voice. Then I got undressed.

The water took me back to a day many years ago, at the beach. I had gone to see Alba at the Lido Delfini. Alba was caught up in the trend for windsurfing, despite having no sense of balance. Lido Delfini is a pretty spot, the triangular sails visible from the seafront and mingling with the flags flapping on the terraces. Today as then. Coloured flags, banners.

Anyway, I was already in the water when Vittoria joined me, or perhaps she didn't join me, she merely swam in my direction. She was floating and trying to tie her bikini top. One of those bandeau ones, with a string you pull to tie it around your neck, transforming the bandeau into a bow stuffed with two breasts. Those bikinis never go out of fashion. Only the string was so tangled up I thought it was a flower. Vittoria swimming with a flower between her breasts. It seemed odd, but that's what I thought. There was something about her I found disturbing, the fleeting colour of her eyes, her sharp but slippery profile, that hesitation in recognising the person she was talking to, as if her mind was elsewhere. The sly smile of a cat ready to pounce on a dragonfly. The sudden high pitch of her voice when she was speaking. And another thing which embarrassed me, when I confessed it to Luigi. I was sensitive to Vittoria's boredom and annoyances. I would like to be bored and annoyed like her.

After she fastened her swimming costume around her neck, Vittoria started swimming again. She went around me, or I went around her. There are no reference points on the beach there. Elsewhere there are a few breakwaters that the sea erodes, winter by winter. But more towards Monte d'Oro, near La Tintarella or Lido del Pino.

How can some people not get their hair wet when they're in the sea? she asked me. It's not the same, she went on, unselfconsciously answering her own question, her eyes some colour midway between the sandy seabed and the sky, yellowed by the wind blowing from Africa. Swimming in the sea isn't like swimming in a river or a lake. No, of course not, I interrupted her hurriedly, lakes are stagnant water. I'd never swum in a river or a lake. I hated repeating things from hearsay, and yet I was doing exactly that, like almost everyone in town.

Stagnant water, repeated Vittoria like an echo, then added Swimming in the sea feels comforting and euphoric. Can you be comforted and euphoric? I asked her, with a hint of annoyance, and Vittoria laughed. It's always comforting to be in the water, and on certain good days, at certain lucky moments, you can feel euphoric too. Then, without adding anything more, she dived and resurfaced every two or three seconds in butterfly stroke, which no one had ever seen or practised before she came to Scauri. At the water's edge I, too, unfastened my bikini top from around my neck and tangled the strings like a bow on a gift.

The memory of Lido Delfini was interrupted by the present memory of Mara's confession. I've been jealous of you.

Was Vittoria euphoric that day at the Lido, while Alba was falling off her windsurfing board? And was I, at least, comforted?

But then I asked myself, as the water rose in the tub, was it true that no one had ever swum butterfly-style, no one had ever drunk cassis, no woman had ever had a boat at the dock? Or had I decided that everything had to begin with Vittoria?

*

I didn't have an accident in my bathtub, and at five minutes to five I walked into Lo Scoglio wearing the white, silver-pinstriped suit I put on when I didn't feel like wearing dark clothes. Tobia, behind the counter, looked up. My own coral-coloured shirt startled me in the mirror behind him. He was drying a beer glass. He gave a jovial jerk of his chin towards one corner, where I turned to see Avvocato Pontecorvo. He was looking at the sea, showing that aquiline profile, his hands folded on the table.

I like people who are punctual, he began, looking at me wide-eyed. I didn't answer, but he suddenly seemed very old and tired to me. That was my favourite corner too.

Why do you reckon it's so hard to wash beer mugs? Tobia asked me, adding, I'll bring you coffee.

The whole beach was in front of us, the Monte d'Argento promontory, the brick-red stain of the Sieci, and the maritime pines, sparse at first then increasingly dense as they formed the pinewoods.

The row of beach clubs, the untidy clumps of houses, the Redeemer promontory which is our own Sugar Loaf Mountain with our own Corcovado Christ. Monte d'Oro, where I buried Madama, who loved sea air. That was behind me. It loomed somehow, like a memory. I thought about the Lido Tahiti but couldn't pick it out, after all it's only a little higher than pavement level. It looked like a wave or a dune, a platform roof over the sea designed by an architect. I thought it looked beautiful. Architects and more architects, like in everything. I looked at the pinewoods again.

Since Gisella Treglia had been killed, the houses in the pinewoods had dropped in value, that's what the property ads were saying. And they have a better memory than people, and sometimes more decency, Luigi would repeat, who thought what he thought about private property but enjoyed seeing me circle ads for houses I would never go and see.

Decaffeinated for me, said Pontecorvo in a different tone, returning to the one with which he had left me, threatening and imperious, in the rectory hallway.

One decaf, please, Tobia, I said, loudly.

I didn't think you were here yet, Avvocato Pontecorvo, I didn't see your car in the car park.

I told Osvaldo to drive around for a while, he'll come back when I ring him. I wanted to surprise you, too.

You flatter me, Avvocato Pontecorvo.

I didn't say it would be a nice surprise.

I kept quiet, staring at the view, until Tobia arrived with the coffees and Pontecorvo, kindly again, asked Sugar?

No thank you. Have you talked to your clients?

The client is my nephew, Avvocato Russo, the son of my sister's daughter, to be precise. The boy admits to throwing the bottle but also says he did not aim at your client's face.

My client, on the other hand, who is no relation of mine, has claimed that your client was drunk and wanted to smash the bottle over his head.

And as Machiavelli teaches us, Avvocato Russo, you have to aim higher to hit a target, so technically my client didn't aim at your client's head but above it.

Are we really going to go on like this?

No, not at all, tell me how much you want.

It's not a question of money, Avvocato Pontecorvo.

Oh, isn't it? What is it then, avvocato? I'm listening.

A way of behaving.

My nephew has never thrown a bottle before, while your client has been in more than one fight, so they say in town. Not to mention the business of the communion wine and wafers.

All right, you've gathered your information, the town's well informed, but, Avvocato Pontecorvo, vox populi is not a witness statement.

But it is a clue, Avvocato Russo, a clue. In any case, the town is not well informed about everything. For example, I can't manage to find out how much my wife paid for those graves, not niches but graves in the ground. Above all, I can't understand why in over twenty years no one has wondered where Vittoria came from and who she was.

And who was she?

My wife.

That seems reductive.

And does fifteen million lire to settle the matter of the bottle and the broken nose seem appropriate to you?

Why all this money, Avvocato Pontecorvo?

Because I would like the matter to be settled here and now, so my boy, who has some excessive behaviour but a lot of potential, and aspires to an international career, can follow his passions and have what he deserves. Because I wouldn't like a little stumble to stain his clean record. And last but not least because I would like to leave this place as soon as possible and never return. Age is on my side in this desire – if one lacks time one must pay, and I am paying. I can pay, and I want to pay.

Avvocato Pontecorvo, I would like your nephew to apologise. Neither you nor I can be certain he hasn't thrown other bottles, and perhaps it would be useful to invite him to reflect on his actions.

He will apologise, Avvocato Russo, although invitations, which are actually obligations, bore me, and educating others bores me too. I don't love myself or like myself so much that I consider myself able to teach anyone anything. In any case, the money we're offering your client is worth more than any apology.

I haven't said I accept.

Your clients won't refuse, believe me.

Don't you take sugar?

No, Signora Russo, I don't take sugar either.

Tobia returned with a plate of biscuits that gave off warmth and a scent of vanilla. No butter and no eggs, he explained.

Cornflour, I said, my mouth full of crumbs.

Incredible as it may seem to you, Vittoria and I loved each other very much.

I had no idea Vittoria was married.

Since she had never asked me for a divorce, I believe she did not intend to.

Would you have agreed to a divorce?

Perhaps not in the late seventies, but by the early eighties, why not?

How long had it been since you'd seen her?

Over ten years.

And had you been in touch recently?

Not in the last five years.

Excuse me asking, Avvocato Pontecorvo, but who told you about the funeral?

A mutual friend, who was told by the woman who lived with Vittoria.

Her name is Mara.

I know her name, Signora Russo. If I don't speak it aloud it's because I don't want to, that name and that woman brought us nothing good.

I don't think Vittoria saw it that way.

I never understood how my wife saw things, but I loved her and I've never remarried.

How could you, avvocato? You weren't divorced, and bigamy is still a crime in this country.

I mean that I would not have remarried in any case, and anyway, I didn't ask for a divorce either, you get married once and for all, even if no one around us seems to remember that. Tell me, Avvocato Russo, why do I have the feeling that I need to ask your permission to take my wife's body home?

As I said, the dead belong to no one, and Rome wasn't the home Vittoria chose.

Synecdoche or metonymy, Signora Russo? Home for me, or I for home? Do you mean to remind me that I wasn't home to Vittoria?

I mean, Avvocato Pontecorvo, that Vittoria's intention was clear, she wanted to stay here, she was a real part of the community, many people relied on her, and not only because she worked in the pharmacy.

She wasn't a pharmacist, Avvocato Russo, Vittoria was one of the first women to graduate with full honours in Medicine at La Sapienza in Rome. She specialised in emergency medicine, then oncology, with a specific interest in radiotherapy. She spent nearly three years in the United States. No, she was no pharmacist, despite my utmost respect for the profession.

It doesn't sound like you mean that.

No, I don't. Think of Homais and Madame Bovary. So can we agree on this money and that nothing happened between these boys? Waiter, the bill.

He's not a waiter, he's the owner, this is a special place. Vittoria always came here after swimming, on Sundays, in summer and in winter. That's her boat there, look. Tobia's not a waiter, he's the owner.

What do you have against waiters, Signora Russo?

Nothing, I was just being precise. I have no facts, Avvocato Pontecorvo, to make me think you and Vittoria loved each other very much, but I have no facts to prove the opposite either. In fact, I imagine that people who have loved each other absolutely can become absolutely indifferent to each other.

Don't overthink it, Avvocato Russo, it's enough that you believe me. The dead, as you said at the rectory and repeated here, belong to no one, but it's only appropriate for the living to speak. Vittoria was an unusual person, otherwise I would not be sitting here after all these years and everything we've been through.

Avvocato Pontecorvo took a mobile phone from his pocket. I'd only seen them in American films about Wall Street. It looked unwieldy but must have worked, because a few minutes after Osvaldo, come and get me, we heard a lively car horn beep outside the door. He got up and I stayed put, transfixed by Vittoria's blue boat.

Signora Russo, I'll expect a call from you by tomorrow.

Of course, avvocato.

Avvocato, if Vittoria left a will, and you have it, I would like to be present when it is opened.

As you know better than I do, death dissolves.

All bonds of matrimony, yes, but she is the woman I married, whom I never divorced, and I would like to be present. Since you like the law so much, I would remind you that I have the right to take the will if I choose.

All right, avvocato, if there is a will I'll let you know. Didn't you say you never wanted to set foot in Scauri again?

Only stupid people never change their mind, isn't that what they say?

He held out a hand, I stood up. He stooped but still towered two heads over me. They must have made a comical couple, he so tall and she so tiny. I sat down again, took off my jacket, and went back to staring at the beach, the autumn light fading more quickly. Tobia came over with an ashtray. Didn't you give up? I asked, taking out a packet and lighter. I took a break, Lea, you take a break, you don't give up. Imagine how stressful, to say I'm giving up. I smiled at Tobia.

We stayed there, smoking, then Tobia, with his blue eyes that turned every woman's head – even my daughters blushed when they went to ask him for a cherry crunch – whispered Lea, is it true that Vittoria was married?

So the lawyer says, Tobi'. And the lawyer is also Vittoria's husband.

What are you talking about, Le', that guy? Ah, did you hear about Anna's son and the bottle?

Of course. They asked me to defend them, but was it a beer bottle?

No, tonic water. Perhaps they were making gin and tonic.

Anyway, the boy who broke Riccardo's nose is the lawyer's nephew, more or less, the lawyer's sister's grandson.

What, are they all related? And people talk about small towns. But do he and Mara know each other?

Apparently, yes.

But you don't know anything?

Not yet.

And what are you going to do?

I don't know, Tobia, I might go home now.

Say hi to Luigi and the girls.

Who knows if Luigi's back?

Do you remember when Filippo's dad died, Lea? On the old road to Penitro. And the dad's brother, who lived there too.

Of course. Uncle Alvise, the one who was blind in one eye.

That's right, him. When Filippo's dad died, Uncle Alvise stayed and lived with his sister-in-law, Filippo's mum, in their house.

I know, I remember, you're not making sense, Tobi'.

I reckon Uncle Alvise and Filippo's mum slept in the same bed, Le'.

They might, but what's that got to do with anything?

That you never know what's going on in someone else's house, sometimes not even in your own house, where you live, let alone in other people's beds.

I started to imagine Vittoria with her husband. We loved each other very much, Avvocato Pontecorvo had said, aggressively. Young, perhaps happy. In comfortable, elegant houses. Family houses. Perhaps with dogs and staff. In that order. Studious, law-abiding, well educated. Both obliged to follow their parents' careers, perhaps. Or perhaps no obligation, a story that began in the cradle. Predestination. Consolidation of roles and heritage. Following in footsteps. Honouring them and going further. And deeper. Her more than him. An only child by choice or misfortune. Older brothers killed in the war, or never born, younger sisters who didn't survive typhoid fever. Or were never born. Either way, carrying on her father's career was down to her, Vittoria. She wanted to or didn't want to. She did it. What did Mara know of all this? And why had Avvocato Pontecorvo said That woman brought us nothing good? The separation, of course, but what else? What had he had to do with them? Did the charge of spousal abandonment persist and subsist for a couple like them, who'd married in another country? London, he'd said. If he'd tried to force her back home, he would have had to come to Scauri. Not once, but many times. It was impossible that no one had seen him around before the funeral. With those cars, which certainly would not go unnoticed. Nor would the driver. Or perhaps Pontecorvo had changed as he grew older. No longer looked the same. No, he looked the same. Is twenty years a lot, or a little? No, they'd have recognised him in town. Or perhaps he hadn't tried to take her home. I couldn't tell whether it was the pain I knew Mara was feeling, or the suspicion that she would tell me nothing, that was pushing me to unravel the thread of this story on my own. A mutual friend told me, Avvocato Pontecorvo had said. Mara and the lawyer had mutual friends. Was he a good man, the pharmacist in *Madame Bovary*, a book I remembered little about?

The tonic water bottle reminded me of the story of the iguana. The summer before Silvia was born.

At the counter of La Tintarella, Mara ordered two tonic waters, wearing a straw hat with a very large brim and a few holes that traced a halo around her head. She waved me over and held out two little bottles, each with a straw, and I looked at her, surprised. The gynaecologist had advised me not to drink fizzy drinks, but while he was explaining the reason for this prohibition, I had been distracted by an ad for a pair of maternity trousers enticing me from the last page of an open magazine. Embarrassed by my lack of attention, I'd simply nodded, reassuring and reassured, and since then observed the rule without exceptions. No fizzy drinks in pregnancy. Later I'd bought two pairs of maternity trousers and never worn them. Luigi teased me about it, saying See? You grew up too close to the church, and he would laugh and kiss me, and then we usually ended up making love with that swelling belly that brought us closer instead of dividing us. So, thinking Mara was offering me a tonic water, I said No thanks. But Mara insisted: Please can you take it to Vittoria, I'm just coming, I have to go to see Filomena, some friends of hers are here from Rome, they're leaving me an iguana for two weeks but I've never looked after one and want to give it back to them alive. Take mine too, I won't be long.

So Mara, with her straw halo, her linen tunic, and her rope sandals, went off and left me with two bottles and straws. I didn't like straws. I didn't know where Vittoria's beach umbrella was, and at the till they told me she was using the Nocellas', the third one down in the first row on the right. Taking care not to trip due to my belly, which obscured my feet, I set off towards the water's edge. Vittoria was reading.

Here we are, she greeted me, smiling.

I held out one of the bottles to her, placing the other on the little table fixed to the beach umbrella.

You drink it, Lea, Mara will be a while with the iguana anyway, you can't drink tonic water warm.

I've never seen an iguana.

I have, many years ago, in Mexico.

I wondered then, and would wonder several times that day, when and why Vittoria had been to Mexico, and now I remembered and asked myself why I stopped wondering. Perhaps Mexico was crucial and I hadn't realised it yet, or never would.

Vittoria moved the bottle closer to me.

No thanks, I can't have fizzy drinks, the gynaecologist advised against it.

But why? she asked, sitting up and discarding her book on the sun lounger. The book assumed the shape of a little tent. She took off her glasses and put one arm in her mouth. The book was small and green. I blushed and said nothing, I didn't know why the gynaecologist had advised against fizzy drinks, so I started digging my toes into the sand. I heard Vittoria stand up. Her shadow reached me before her hand did, grabbing my chin. He'll be worried, quite rightly, about excess sugar, she said. Fizzy drinks contain sugar, but this is tonic water. If you want it, drink it. She held my face and looked me in the eyes. Her fingers were cool. Then she let go of my chin and passed me the bottle. Without taking my eyes off her, my face orphaned of her fingers, I put the straw in my mouth and started sucking. Vittoria went back to the lounger and stared at nothing. I could see that untidy nothingness of wild plants on the sand too. She sat facing away from me and she was quiet, occasionally passing a hand over her back, briefly. I looked at her ringless fingers and thought about my mother's skin, lighter than hers, marked by time, and my mother's hands, ruined by working the land. I looked at her rounded shoulders, her slightly curved back, her golden, bronzed skin, I thought of her cool fingers on the scalding sand. Sonia's voice, repeating Vittoria is kind of sexy. Then, absent-mindedly, I sucked again and the bottle reverberated with an ambiguous wet sound. The tonic water was finished. Vittoria turned to me, laughing. She picked up her little green book and said As soon as the baby's born and Pietro really leaves me the boat, we'll take him out on the sea. I blushed, but perhaps it was the heat rising from my toes in the fiery sand. It's unbelievable, she went on, that the children in this town only experience the sea from the land, or occasionally a pedalo. Then she added All right then. The dismissal, the end of all conversations, that everyone in town had learned to recognise.

That night I woke up and repeated it: All right then. Several times. First resignedly, then angrily. Luigi went on sleeping, and perhaps that's what annoyed me. Somewhat inconsiderately, I went and shut myself in the bathroom to smoke. Outside the window, the moon lit up our neighbour's vegetable plot, where a ginger cat was curled up next to a pumpkin no one had picked but which hadn't made up its mind to rot. What did I know about Vittoria? That she was married, that she had been a doctor and had stopped practising, that she had moved to Scauri from Rome and various other places where she had studied and practised her profession, and that she had lived the last twenty plus years of her life with Mara. That she had been to the United States and Mexico, and got married in London. Mara had brought nothing good. I couldn't get Mara's voice out of my head, saying that they had made love on Saturday night. Pontecorvo's voice hissing That woman brought us nothing good, and my voice remembering They were lovers. Like that, to get myself out of the way at least, I whispered it, exhaling it along with the smoke: They were lovers. And that's when I understood. Understanding was like a weight between my legs, and in the effort of keeping my balance I didn't hear Luigi coming in.

Aren't you feeling well, Lea?

What are you doing, following me? Leave me alone.

You're tense. What's happened?

We shouldn't have gone to Ponza, and then today there was Vittoria's funeral.

So they told me.

Who?

Some Romans.

She was married.

They told me.

And what else did they tell you?

Nothing you don't already know, but the body has to stay here.

Father Michele gave me her will.

What's in it?

I didn't open it, I wanted to give it to Mara.

But Father Michele gave it to you.

The husband asked me if he can be present when the will's opened.

You met the husband?

They didn't tell you that then? It's the juiciest bit. Vittoria's husband is the lawyer of that Roman boy who threw a bottle at the ironmonger's son's head.

What are you talking about?

It's true. Luigi, why do you think no one's picked that pumpkin?

What pumpkin? Oh, I hadn't noticed it, it looked like a ginger cat.

I went over and hugged him, the heat of his body with the warmth of the blankets he had emerged from.

They were lovers, those two, they made love.

I should hope they did, Le'.

Did you ever think about it?

I don't know, perhaps at first. When they arrived here it wasn't clear, we all wondered. But I wasn't always here. First the army, then Frascati and the Party. I'm more interested in what I love, not what other people do.

But you're the biggest gossip of anyone.

I didn't think about it, no, I don't remember thinking about Vittoria and Mara in bed together.

Didn't you ever find it weird that two women of such different ages lived together without being related?

Lea, there are loads of people here who live together without being related or married.

I feel stupid.

Why?

Mara told me she'd been jealous of me, she says Vittoria liked me.

And you never noticed?

No, but I never even thought about it.

Why are you feeling this way, Le'?

Because Vittoria's dead, because she told the priest to give me the will, because I feel like women never did anything here before Vittoria, because in the Polaroid photo, the one that group of troublemakers took while the others were headbutting and glassing each other, you can see Vittoria walking.

What do you mean?

In the Polaroid from Saturday, Vittoria was alive and walking, and on Sunday morning she had a swim at the cliffs, a coffee with Carmela from Ernesto Bruno, and then died.

We're all alive until the second before we kick the bucket, Le'.

She can't have died by accident in her own bathtub.

But the autopsy showed nothing, apart from water in her lungs, and anyway, what motive would anyone have for killing her?

What if she killed herself?

What reason did she have to kill herself, Le'? She was loved, she was happy, her home was full of people, the town don't want her remains to be sent away, she was a celebrity. Now you're telling me she even had a shag on Saturday night.

What if she really did fancy me?

Why are you obsessing about this now? There's something going on that I don't get, and anyway, we'll never know, Lea, my love, Vittoria's dead.

And what if I fancied her?

Did you fancy Vittoria?

I don't know.

And you'll never know, Lea, my love, Vittoria's dead.

But I have to know, Luigi, I'm alive.

Luigi went back to bed, snorting, and I started staring at the woman in the mirror. I couldn't superimpose the image of myself sitting happily, holding the girls in my arms, in the photo I kept in the kitchen, over the one of me in the water staring at the string flower in the gap between Vittoria's breasts. I couldn't decide if that was the same woman, in that fading snapshot, and in that memory that was getting distorted. So I went back into the living room as the sky turned from blue to indigo, to get Vittoria's will from my bag. I imagined I would justify it to myself in the following days by saying I did what I was about to do as if in a trance, like a sleepwalker. I cobbled together terms, justifying my actions before making them. If someone asked, I would say I was in a state of confusion, and that confusion was due to profound emotion. I glimpsed the ribbon of a possible and unrealised life unravelling beside me, light and misunderstood like a Lycra flower between breasts. I remembered the fabric flowers Vittoria pinned to her jumpers and shirts. Below the neck but above the heart. Red or maroon in a sea of dove grey, blue, off-white, sand, light and air-force blue, mustard. At sea. I took the will, certain that the sealed envelope contained a letter for me. I wanted there to be one. I longed for that message from beyond the grave, even more than I had longed for my daughters, or so it seemed. I looked at the envelope. I no longer recognised myself, I wanted someone to tell me who I was. Kiss, letter, will, as the Italian nursery rhyme goes.

Going into the kitchen, I put water on the stove and waited for it to boil. Then, like in the *Junior Woodchucks' Guidebook*, which I had just given Silvia, I held the envelope above the steam and waited for the heat to melt the glue and soften the sealing wax. It didn't take long.

I realised at once that I'd never seen Vittoria's handwriting. Was it hers? Would her husband ask for an expert opinion? Would we have to compare it to the pharmacy registers?

Vittoria had left everything in the house to Mara, she wanted her friends to take something of hers, and the boat, should Mara not want to take care of it, was to remain at the disposal of the dock until Vittorio was old enough to decide whether he was interested in it or not. Half the money in her current account at the Banca di Roma in the Via Appia went to Mara and half to the railwaymen's club. Lastly, she thanked me for agreeing to read these lines and asked me to make sure that a small head by Canova, the plaster sculpture I had always seen in her living room but whose provenance

I had never questioned and which, according to the will, was a Sibyl – hence the dog's name, perhaps – should be left to Rebecca, and to remind Mara of this. The post scriptum was for Pontecorvo, reiterating that he had already had everything he was entitled to, a strange formula.

I stared at the tiles above the stove which were always a bit greasy and shiny. It wasn't a letter to me, it was a will. Instructions. Who was Rebecca, the one who was to have the Sibyl head? Rebecca, with no surname and no other address. Rebecca, who had inherited a Canova plaster. I had to read out her wishes and that's all. I was curious about Pontecorvo's reaction. I looked at the sheet of paper against the light, then I said, All right then. I resealed the envelope and put it back in my bag. I could see my fingerprints on the sealing wax, but perhaps it was just the fear of having to explain to someone what I had done. I wanted one of Vittoria's jumpers at least.

The phone call with Pontecorvo was curt. He assured me that he would come to my office about three o'clock, and almost gallantly emphasised that he was sure to be on time, despite the forty-eight steps. I don't know why, but as I put down the receiver I wondered whether those rooms, in a nice little early-twentieth-century building between a pizzeria and a perfume shop, would be suitable to receive a man like Avvocato Pontecorvo. Perhaps I should ask some colleague from Formia or Gaeta, with more prestigious and established offices, to let me use them. I've always been more uneasy than insecure. Questions I had forgotten asking myself would resurface during the day. I didn't really know who I was, or who Vittoria had been, and no matter how I tried not to connect these things, I knew there was a link. Also, I hated Thursdays, such a bland day. I didn't like the name either. I felt guilty for ringing Avvocato Pontecorvo before Mara. Was I jealous of Mara? I couldn't accept that she knew everything about Vittoria and I knew nothing.

Like in fairy tales, where everyone does not always live happily ever after, the phone rang. My secretary, Cristina, would be there in a few minutes and I answered, aware of who would be at the other end of the phone.

I was hoping you'd already be in the office.

I was about to ring you. Father Michele gave me Vittoria's will.

She'd made a will? Did she know she was going to die?

No, I don't think so. Father Michele says she gave it to him over six months ago, out of superstition.

Vittoria wasn't superstitious.

I wouldn't have said so either, but that's what Father Michele claims.

That can't be it, Lea, you could say many things about Vittoria but not that she was superstitious. Fatalistic, yes, superstitious, no.

I didn't know her that well, Mara, in fact yesterday at the funeral I realised I knew absolutely nothing about Vittoria.

We knew what Vittoria wanted us to know about Vittoria.

You too?

Yes, Lea, me too.

And her husband?

She always told me it was a great love affair.

And why did it end?

I should have asked her that when I had the chance, but I didn't.

And you and her?

A great love affair.
Mara's voice was suddenly happy, light.

All great love affairs.

The door to my room was open, so I heard the key in the lock and saw Cristina come in. She smiled at me, weighed down with bags as usual. She went shopping before coming to the office. The smell of bananas bothered me.
Lea?
I have the will here, Mara, I wanted to open it this afternoon. I'll have to let Avvocato Pontecorvo know.
Oh, will you?
He's her husband. Her widower, in fact. They never divorced.
Do what you have to do, Lea, but he had nothing more to do with Vittoria, and I don't think his name will be mentioned in those documents.
That's exactly why it's better if he's present.
Perhaps you're right.
What did you want to tell me?
Come and choose something from her clothes. She was smaller than you, but we'll find something.
Thanks.
Like I said, she really liked you.
Sounds of a domestic jungle came from the receiver: dogs barking, cats meowing, birds singing, and at one point a voice called Mara twice, the first time clearly, the second time muffled, a hand placed over the receiver.

Who's that? I asked, offended, as if I'd surprised a thief in the house.

Filomena, Mara answered. I asked her to sleep here, I couldn't be alone.

Where?

What kind of a question is that?

Sorry, I don't know what kind of question it is. I'll be round in the afternoon, say hello to Filomena.

Lea?

Yes?

What kind of a question is that?

Nothing, Mara love, the old insidious habit of asking questions that makes you ask meaningless ones, sorry.

Cristina brought me my coffee and a brioche from Vezza's, the kind I liked best. I didn't know much about Filomena Paradiso, of the funeral parlour of the same name. Perhaps she was married, perhaps she had children, and she definitely ran the business her grandfather had started and her father had consolidated. If she had children I would know, because they would be more or less the same age as mine. Or perhaps they were younger, or older enough to be invisible to me. Usually, if you don't hear anything in town, nothing has happened.

She would certainly have taken care of Vittoria and Mara's graves, but when? Had she suggested it to Vittoria, or had Vittoria herself come forward? My grandmother, my father's mother, had sent me to Minturno to buy two burial niches, one for her and one for Nonno, when I was ten. Nonna had been sixty-one then. Younger than Vittoria and already thinking about her coffin. The cemetery space was state-owned, but the funeral directors had privileged access. Vittoria had probably asked Filomena herself. I couldn't imagine a conversation between Filomena and Vittoria.

I smiled at the thought of what Luigi would say about privileged access to graves or niches. Welcome to Paradiso, do you want the third or the seventh row? You'll have a view of the whole gulf. Or perhaps you'd prefer to sleep in this soft earth, enriched with centuries and centuries of bloated corpses and carcasses. Apparently the cemetery was already here in the pre-Roman age, when the Volsci or Cimbri peoples roamed across this area. Not that I could remember which populations had reached our shores, but studying with the girls had refreshed my memory. Or perhaps there were things we didn't study at all when I was at school.

The idea of Filomena and Mara in the same bed felt weird to me. Mara was curvy, Filomena so thin she looked like the woman with the scythe who provided her with a living. Mara always half-dressed, Filomena always overdressed. Even in summer. When even the salty sea air failed to mask the fusty smell that hung around her like a lame but loyal dog.

Did she wash herself to get into bed with Mara? And had Vittoria known about this friendship? Or was it just an affair, cuckold's horns? Both sides can cheat. The plaster Sibyl. The Canova head has horns. The dog named Sibilla has ears.

Meanwhile my own head was running wild and getting lost like children who go off exploring the surroundings and call heaps of pozzolanic ash mountains, and irrigation ditches chasms. Everything they see becomes huge when they talk about it, they have adventures and invent names for all the things they don't know. I discovered capacities for speculation in myself that I had believed dormant, the possibility of autosuggestion that is a resource in childhood and a nasty vice in adults. All my university lecturers had pointed it out to me, in more or less aggravating ways. Avvocato, they would say, you have too fertile an imagination. At the University of Naples, they called you avvocato as soon as you crossed the threshold of Via Mezzocannone, perhaps they still do. Drawling out the second syllable and giving you the notion that someone already sees you down the polished corridor of a courthouse, victorious after a trial.

Perhaps it was that sensation of past and victory that brought me back to the will, and that evocative, outdated name, Rebecca, written in its lines. Unable to remain in my seat, intimidated by the bundles of papers and files piled up on my desk, I went out. It was a lovely sunny day. I was like my daughter Giulia, who, having spent endless minutes in front of the ice cream counter and carefully chosen three flavours, strawberry, chocolate, and lemon, would sit primly on the bench, her feet not touching the ground, and stir and stir with the little spoon in the tub, mixing all the flavours together before eating them.

*

The ironmonger's shop owned by Riccardo's father was in the old market square. Walking at a brisk pace, I turned into the street after the Via Appia branch of the Banco di Roma, leading down to the sea. I'd always liked the little square, shaded by maritime pines whose powerful roots broke the monotony of the tarmac. The street that led down from the Via Appia opened out into the square and continued to the seafront. I had taken Silvia there to explain the difference between outflow and inflow when she was studying rivers and tributaries came up.

The narrow street led between the Polish nuns' convent and the sports centre. Pope Wojtyła had stayed with the Polish nuns. I hadn't liked him because he passed himself off as a progressive, which he wasn't. The nuns' garden reached down to the seafront. On the gate it said STELLA MARIS in wrought iron. An uncle of Luigi's had welded and beaten that gate. Every time I stopped by to say hello, he would promise to make me four chairs and a table for the garden. The sea was grey, the beach clubs in hibernation, the opaque oleanders swayed like dancers in chains, a dog barked from the beach. Luigi's uncle never had made me the chairs, nor a table.

Riccardo's father, who was a few years older than Luigi and had also attended the technical institute in Bagnoli, but not finished it, was serving a woman who I thought was the mother or sister of the frozen food delivery guy. I concentrated on the screwdrivers.

Luigi had two toolboxes which he was very possessive about and which he did not want me to touch. They were probably the only places he took care to keep perfectly tidy. Otherwise he was a careless man. He never pushed chairs back under the table, or closed drawers. He would fill a jug of water, spill half of it, and walk in the puddles, leaving footprints throughout the house. We laughed at him for being careless. When I went to the Bar Association to tell them I was expecting Giulia, my colleagues congratulated me and, I don't know why, I said My husband's careless. We all burst out laughing.

Occasionally, holding a daughter on each thigh, Luigi would say Thank goodness Dad's careless, and we would all four of us laugh, and I was happy. I was happy to have the girls. I was happy to have married a man who has a thousand faults but the great virtue of never saying a word about the state of the house, or whether food is on the table, or the time I spend out for work. It has never bothered him. It doesn't matter to him whether I behave like a wife, but I think he likes being a husband. I keep closing drawers, pushing chairs under the table, drying the footprints, almost always with a certain lightness of heart. And let's hope I always do.

Avvocato Russo, do you need something?

I came about Riccardo.

Have you talked to the big lawyer from Rome?

Yes, yesterday afternoon.

And what did he say?

He's offering fifteen million lire to settle everything and say no more about it.

Fifteen million?

Yes, fifteen million.

I don't know how much you and Luigi earn, avvocato, it takes me nearly a year to put together fifteen million. Sure, it's better in summer, but I don't earn more than three or four hundred thousand lire a month.

I know it's a lot, Angelo, but I also know that if we do this we're letting him get away with something that could have had more serious consequences.

Yes, but nothing happened in the end, and then you said that stuff about minors and criminal records.

Riccardo has a broken nose, but it could have been his head.

But it wasn't his head that got smashed open like a melon, Le'. I'll tell Anna, but I reckon we'll accept. Suppose Riccardo starts studying and wants to go to university in Rome, or start a business, who knows? Who's ever seen fifteen million all at once? When Anna and I got married, we got six hundred thousand from all our relatives put together.

I get it, that was '76, it wasn't so little then.

Wasn't much either, Le'.

I'd have liked to steal a screwdriver for Luigi, but instead I said goodbye and went back to the Via Appia. How money could change the intention to warn outsiders against aggressive behaviour. How much had money come into Vittoria and Mara's relationship, or Vittoria's with her husband? I could clearly remember the expensive clothes worn by the people who got out of those expensive cars. Models in fashion magazines. I could imagine their bodies under their clothes, wearing underwear from Ernesto Bruno that I couldn't or wouldn't afford. I thought about my cotton pants, Luigi's pants, the girls', and their ribbed vests.

What kind of pants had Vittoria worn, and how had she taken them off? First one leg, then the other? Did she pull them off in one go, like Luigi, naked in one step, beyond the double ring of fabric? I was thinking about other people's pants too much, so I went to the newsagent's to distract myself and asked for *L'Unità*. Communists like Luigi didn't like talking aloud about pants. I also voted communist but didn't mind flicking through the pages of shopping catalogues.

While I was paying, I was distracted by noises in the room at the back of the newsagent's, where there were three public telephones and phone directories for many cities and provinces in Italy. Two children ran out. As they often did, they'd sneaked into the little room and taken the receivers off the hook. Children dismantle the world, children are mischievous as monkeys. I would repeat that thing about monkeys to my daughters, although the only monkey I'd ever seen, at the zoo in Rome, hadn't been mischievous at all. On the contrary it sat there, like a poised and stand-offish matron, peeling bananas and eating them in a single mouthful. Alba had nicknamed it the Duchesse de Guermantes of monkeys.

We liked reading Proust, and more generally books that had never found their way into our own homes. For this reason I liked almost all books. Alba had more books at home, but not that many, because her parents had made their money selling fish.

The Duchesse de Guermantes of monkeys watched apathetically as children and adults threw peanuts. As I headed towards the telephone directories I suppressed the suspicion that that memory, too, was of a sexual nature. At our friends' weddings, someone always offered the groom a plate with half a peach garnished with a sprig of parsley, and the bride a plate with a banana and two apricots, or chestnut burrs, depending on the season. I preferred peaches, in any case.

I grabbed the double volume for Rome City and Province, and sat down. I took out my notebook and fountain pen, a gift from my parents when I graduated, and started looking for Rebeccas. I felt sure Rebecca was not married and had a phone. The pen was black and shiny like the pendulum my parents used to look for illnesses and flaws.

A mutual friend told me, Avvocato Pontecorvo had said. Mara must have called the mutual friend.

They must all have used the phone. However, after twenty minutes I had only glanced through ten pages, and although I was quick with lists, tables of numbers, names, and car number plates, I realised this was too long a route, however reliable it might be. Either the fountain pen didn't work as well as the pendulum, or I was no good.

In my office, I found a note on my desk from Anna, Riccardo's mother, saying they were ready to accept Avvocato

Pontecorvo's offer. I wondered why he wanted to pay so much, and why they – more or less aware of their son's character – wanted to accept. I took the Polaroid out of the drawer and looked at it again. It had nothing new to tell me. But Vittoria, walking in the background, was more in focus than the boys in the foreground.

Often, when Vittoria met me in the street, she would take my arm. We would walk along the Via Appia, stopping occasionally to look at shop windows, or someone would say hello and exchange a few words.

Sometimes we would walk the long way home, taking the villa road down to the seafront and coming back up along the one that flanked the primary school. We would separate at the Via Olivella traffic lights, I would go in and she would go back as far as Via Romanelli. Sometimes she stopped to drink a Kir at Bar Haiti. Other times, we drank one together.

What did we talk about? She liked flowers, leaves, herbs, shells, boats. Boats she liked very much, ships too. She liked the dock and Lo Scoglio, she liked palm trees and oleanders. She liked baked fish, train carriages, especially restaurant carriages, sea urchins, the sea, walking in unfamiliar cities, dogs, cats, sassy children, the sun through leaves, bars, card games, and Coca-Cola. She liked straws.

We often talked about history, because she was interested in history and so was I. I wondered how many of the things Vittoria loved were in Scauri, and I told myself none, except for the sea, baked fish, coloured straws, and sea urchins when it was the season.

I attended nursery and reception year at the nuns' and learned, as many did, to walk with linked arms. I'm not sure if I learned it, but I did it out of habit. Then I lost the habit, and no longer did it with any of my friends. With Vittoria I did, perhaps due to the difference in generation. Actually, my mother used to link arms with me too. Once I met Vittoria outside the primary school, just standing there, the white hairs starting to appear on her head and glinting in the sun, watching a group of little kids getting ready to come out of school, perhaps for a trip. Unsmiling, with her quick sandy eyes, Vittoria was looking at the children's hands, all clinging to a single scarf. The teacher had probably told them to stay put, and invented the trick of the piece of material. Like this, those children looked like the thousand feet of a millipede. I called her, and, turning, she waved at me.

You know, she said, I haven't seen anything like that since I was at nursery school. The nuns made us walk like that.

She didn't say anything else, and I didn't ask which nuns, which school, where this happened, who her classmates were, and not because I wasn't curious but because Vittoria pre-empted me at once. Let's go, she said, I'll walk to your office with you. She asked about Luigi, the girls, my parents, and I talked, talked, talked, sometimes even bad-mouthing, complaining, and the answers ranged from a smile to a laugh, or some exclamation of amusement or displeasure.

Vittoria linked arms with me, squeezed my wrist, put a hand around my waist and pulled me to her as if to shake me or rock me. She touched me, caressed me, her hands commented even when she wasn't speaking to me. One has to say something during married life, no? Yes, I answered, yes, of course.

I never knew anything about her, only what she did in Scauri. And in the end I didn't even know that from her own lips. Now I see that Vittoria became a part of the town's mythology, and that mythology, which seemed spontaneous, may have been brought about by Vittoria herself. By her sobriety, her reticence in commenting on facts with words. Vittoria didn't talk much, but she was enthusiastic in her shyness. And in saying so little, she was different from us. She came from somewhere else. Even more than Big Lina, the pharmacist. From homes with books, from being accustomed to receptions and chatter, to journeys, from a history that didn't concern us, full of the past tenses of those who write history. I love couchettes and restaurant carriages.

We were poor people, to use an expression of Luigi's mother's, and Vittoria was not. I wondered what she thought of us. Perhaps, since Mara was of our kind, she liked us. She had chosen us. She wanted to seduce us all. But why?

I wonder if I would have done the same, in Vittoria's shoes, or if it had been her choice. Or if it had just happened. Or if she'd had to hide. Vittoria's death revealed to us what had been clear to her: that is, that we knew nothing about her.

When Avvocato Pontecorvo came I was still thinking about the phone directory. About what I would say if I phoned all the Rebeccas in Rome. About how many Rebeccas there were in Rome. Luigi always played the game with the girls of how many piano tuners there were in New York State. How many tuners are there in New York State? Silvia and Giulia would laugh, and I would think.

I must have looked dispirited, because when the old man asked permission to enter and sat down, he said Avvocato Russo, you don't look too well. I watched him tidy his hair, smooth it down on the back of his neck.

We waited in silence for Mara to arrive, hypnotised by the ticking of the clock.

I hadn't seen Vittoria for almost ten years, and I didn't see her dead body. Did she look the same?

I met Vittoria twenty-odd years ago, I don't know what she was like before. Her hair had been white for a while, for the rest she looked the same as when I met her.

I'd have liked to see her, she's a woman I loved.

I don't think I can ask you what happened.

In the end, Avvocato Russo, I couldn't tell you, I think she simply got tired. Vittoria couldn't stand boredom, her own or others'.

Do people split up because they're bored, Avvocato Pontecorvo?

Yes, people like Vittoria can leave everything they have for a lot less than boredom, or they can stay, in spite of being bored or feeling obliged to. But I think she chose to leave because we loved each other very much.

There's something about this business I don't understand.

And why should you, Avvocato Russo? You're still too young to accept that some things are impossible to understand.

It's just that I know I passed close to Vittoria in the last twenty years, Avvocato Pontecorvo, and hardly saw her. I feel like I missed an opportunity. I'm sorry, but before I forget – it is the reason we're meeting, after all – my clients accept the money you are offering to settle the matter of the fight.

I hope the boy's face isn't too swollen.

I hope your nephew learns something from this affair.

Why should he?

I don't know, I just hope he does.

It's strange to hear hope coming from a lawyer's lips, isn't it? Will we have to wait much longer for the woman who lived with my wife?

I'm sorry you didn't even see Vittoria dead.

I'm almost dead too, Avvocato Russo. If I concentrate I can imagine her.

How did your paths cross ten years ago?

By chance. It seemed odd to see her in the street and not call out to her.

And did you call out to her?

Yes.

And what did Vittoria do?

She smiled and waved her hand, ciao-ciao, then she walked off without turning back. Did she still wave her hand like that?

Yes, sometimes she would blow me a kiss, put her hand to her lips and smack a kiss.

She must have liked you, Avvocato Russo, and since that's so, I'll tell you how the story of the taxi went and not how I would have liked it to go, which is what I told you a few seconds ago. I would have liked it to be Vittoria's fault yet again.

What do you mean, yet again?

Never mind. I was waiting for a taxi, I saw her and called to her. Vittoria waved her hand at me, she was about to cross the road. I was in Corso Vittorio near Via dei Baullari, and she was coming from Piazza Navona, but the taxi pulled up and I got in, and I saw her still looking at the car, but I couldn't lower the tinted windows. I would have said Get in, I'll give you a lift, but the window stayed shut. Time was ticking, and I felt embarrassed for both of us. I didn't even tell the taxi driver. A moment. Still. Nothing. And the taxi drove off.

I felt almost certain the lawyer was going to cry, but instead, when the patter of footsteps outside the door drowned out the chimes of the clock that had marked out our halting revelations, Pontecorvo whipped around as quickly as a snake, his eyes snake-like too. He stood up.

Avvocato, no need to stand, it's my office, not yours.

I'm still a gentleman, Signora Russo, I stand up for a lady, even a lady who, as I told you, brought us bad luck.

Calm down, Avvocato Pontecorvo.

Mind what you're saying, Avvocato Russo.

I'm not the one getting worked up.

You don't know what happened.

Tell me.

If Vittoria didn't talk about it, neither will I, and I hope no one else will either.

Mara was accompanied by Filomena. She was wearing a teenage-style dress, stylishly patched, too summery even for this mild October. I'd never seen her wear it before. Avvocato Pontecorvo must also have been troubled by thoughts about the dress, because his eyes lingered on it until Mara sat down. Filomena stood behind her, her hands on the backrest of the chair. A rough copy of an early-twentieth-century family photo, the black-and-white ones, with the men standing, the women sitting, and a background of draped fabric. All that was missing was the ghost.

I was disgusted by what I was thinking.

I despised Filomena, feared her perhaps. She had insinuated herself into the relationship between Vittoria and Mara. Greed makes the world go round. Vittoria died in the bathtub for no reason. Where had Filomena Paradiso, of the funeral parlour of the same name, been on Sunday morning? Had she gained more from Vittoria's death than the money for the funeral? Does it take courage to kill someone, or is envy enough? Did Filomena envy Vittoria and Mara, want to be them? Omnia munda mundis, as Fra' Cristoforo would say, and my mother would repeat to me. She didn't know Latin but acted according to the precept that to the pure all things are pure. Where would I find Rebecca's surname? What significance did the Sibyl head have, if any? Was Vittoria superstitious? And what was the meaning of that story about the taxi, Pontecorvo, and Vittoria?

Avvocato Pontecorvo's voice interrupted my questions, but not my suspicions.

Avvocato Russo, can we read this will or must we wait longer?

Mara didn't speak, didn't answer, she smoothed the frill of her skirt. Her hair was loose. I recognised the ringlets that had previously been braids.

I leave all the contents of the house to Mara Amadasi. I would like my friends to take something, if they want to. I leave the boat to Mara Amadasi with the request that she wait until Vittorio De Filippis decides whether he will keep it or not, when he is of an appropriate age, and I trust that should Mara Amadasi sell it, she will offer the dock first refusal. I leave half the money in my current account in the Banca di Roma, Via Appia 128, to Mara Amadasi, and half to the railwaymen's club.

Lastly, I thank Avvocato Lea Russo for agreeing to read these lines and request that she remind Mara Amadasi that the Canova plaster belongs to Rebecca.

I am sure Giorgio Pontecorvo d'Aquino, who would also have the right to half of what I possess, has nothing to claim, knowing he has already had what he is entitled to.

There's nothing more, not even Rebecca's surname, I said, raising my eyes and finding the two people in front of me holding their breath as if it was a competition. There's nothing more, I repeated, replacing the paper in the envelope. I don't know what expression was on Filomena's face.

May I have that envelope as a personal memento? Also because I imagine I may not come and take so much as a matchstick.

Giorgio. Mara spoke, and her voice seemed to come from somewhere else in the room, from outside in the street, in fact somewhere beyond the window. If Vittoria had wanted you to have something, she'd have written it down, but instead she took the trouble to point out that you've had what you're entitled to. Having said that, if you want to come to my house and take a matchstick, you may.

Mara stood up and left, followed by Filomena. She didn't say goodbye, she made no sound. She joined her voice outside.

I had better go, Signora Russo, thank you for everything.

Take the letter if you're interested, I won't do anything with it and nor will Mara, I only need a photocopy just in case.

Thank you for your kindness, and if you should need the original, though I don't see why you should, you can always have it back.

Who's Rebecca?

A woman who, I now realise, looks a little like you. Typical of Vittoria, something as a consolation for something else. Living on surrogates, what a great skill it is to recognise that in oneself. Anyway, my office will write to you about the matter of the two boys.

I would like them to meet and talk, Avvocato Pontecorvo.

I have no objection, but I'd prefer to settle the paperwork first, there's plenty of time for chit-chat.

It's not chit-chat.

You women are all the same.

I don't respond to provocation.

It is not provocation, it is the truth, you are all the same.

So you are saying I and Rebecca look alike?

Incredible as it may be, you and Rebecca Lanza do look alike.

And who is Rebecca Lanza?

Avvocato, if Vittoria had wanted you, or anyone else in this dump where she retreated with her broken doll in a torn dress to know Rebecca, you would have met her, but you did not, and therefore I will not introduce her either. Goodbye, it has not been unpleasant talking to you, you have my telephone numbers.

And you have mine.

He touched the brim of his hat and left.

All the world that interested me was now outside the window.

Listen to me, Lea. Vittoria went away a month after she turned forty-three. I had organised a wonderful party for her. A lot of people. Until then, I had thought she liked people. Instead, from the next morning, perhaps from that very night, she never came back to sleep in our bedroom. Something had changed. A crease of disgust had appeared on her face. As if she had been drunk, and drunkenness and excess had annoyed her. I myself annoyed her. Out of the blue. I had organised everything, but it wasn't a surprise party. She had told me that since she was twenty-five, she had been looking forward to turning forty. She had always hated menstruating. Vittoria was like that, or at least she had been until that day. Let's have a party for my forty-third birthday. Not forty, not fifty. Forty-three. She was a rather original woman. She liked bodies, all bodies. We celebrated every year. I loved her and I remember what she desired or said she desired. I don't know what your relationship is with your husband, but there was a complicity between Vittoria and me. We liked the same things. The same people. I'm not speaking broadly. The same things. The same people. We were complicit. I'm celebrating because I'm leaving menstruation behind, well, almost, I'm closer to the end than the beginning, I'm leaving behind the obligation to seduce or be seduced. Consider me free. I think seduction was Vittoria's main practice. A practice repeated so often it became natural. Despite growing up in this place of junk and rubbish bags in the street and the stink of vermin, of seasonal rentals for people like you but who happened to be born and live nowhere near the sea, you will have realised that Vittoria was irresistible? Or were you immune to her? No, not you, Avvocato Russo, I recognise the fever. And I recognise something else, in your features. However, something must have happened at that party, which was like so many other parties, so many other evenings. Something, or someone. And I have never managed to get an explanation. I begged and threatened, I had her tailed and I tried to buy her off, but I never managed to get Vittoria's own authentic explanation, nothing. I'm not stupid, but I don't understand. It may be that Signora Amadasi, who was at the party, knows what happened, and if so, I also know Signora Amadasi will tell me nothing, because the only thing I ever managed to get Vittoria to tell me is that I didn't know when to stop and was therefore damned. You can't distinguish between games, between blessings and curses. Nicely put, wasn't it? Vittoria expressed herself well. Suddenly damned, I'll say it again, for things that had happened dozens of times before, and which my lady wife had shrugged off, merely lighting a cigarette. Changing the rules of the game while the game is being played. Doesn't that bother you? It's impossible. It's unfair. I don't trust it. You're damned but I can still save myself, and I will. That's what she told me. I don't believe she was interested in salvation, or perhaps she was. I didn't believe her, obviously, it was something else. Or perhaps for Vittoria salvation was a person. She could still save herself, and she would, she kept saying. Save yourself, what can I tell you? Or save someone else. From what, by the way, since it was all paid for? So the key to this damnation must still be inside Signora Amadasi. Many things have been inside Signora Amadasi, by the way. If someone was saved in this whole story, it was neither Vittoria nor myself. I came back to tell you this, Avvocato Russo, to try and dissuade you. Don't look for anything, don't ask questions, don't stir up dust that has hardened into the consistency of a wall. Don't feel too bad about it: if I survived this impossibility of understanding, if I accepted exclusion from the life of the woman with whom I had shared desires until then, then it's possible for everyone to accept everything, and above all, to accept only being able to love in a mediocre way, and avoid taking a fancy to people, because that's what this is in your case, Avvocato Russo, taking a fancy to people like Vittoria, whose first instinct is to say nothing. I'm speaking to you as a father, although I don't have children. Above all, I'm speaking as a man, and in a way I'm giving you a legal opinion, too, which you have not asked for. Don't stir up lives that have nothing to do with yours, and to which you are not equal, because although you may have the talent for it, you have neither the character nor the habit.

At home, Luigi was cooking rice in broth, which the girls liked because it was cooked in the oven. A sort of pilaf rice that had become a family tradition. Anastasia Romanov's rice. I'd given them a book about the tsars. I could hear Silvia and Giulia playing with their dolls in the other room. Their voices reached me, intent on making up a story set in the rainforest. They didn't run to greet me as usual, and I didn't go into the bedroom.

I took the opportunity for some peace and quiet.

Luigi poured me half a glass of red wine, adding that it wasn't my father's. Drink it, it won't kill you, he said. Outside the window the medlar tree was luxuriant, although it was winter. Dark green. Its horny leaves bothered me, they were like turtles or intertwined bodies. The medlar leaves were naked. The dress Mara had worn that afternoon revealed her thighs. Luigi put the casserole dish in the oven and sat with me. The broken doll with the torn dress.

Anna rang, Riccardo's mum, she says you didn't stop by, and she asked for you in the office this afternoon but Cristina said you were busy.

She'll want to make it clear they accept Avvocato Pontecorvo's money to settle the matter of the fight.

I told her you'd call her back.

I will, Luigi, I've already settled the bottle incident. I read Vittoria's will to Mara and Avvocato Pontecorvo.

And what was in it?

Nothing we didn't expect, everything goes to Mara, friends can take something they'd like, except a Canova plaster which is for someone called Rebecca Lanza.

A collector, a princess?

Who knows.

Imagine the girls faced with Princess Lanza. Forget Anastasia.

I don't think the princess will ever come to Scauri.

So Vittoria had a Canova plaster in her house?

Apparently so.

But who is this Rebecca?

I've no idea.

And Mara and Pontecorvo didn't say anything?

I didn't ask Mara, also because she came with Filomena.

Filomena Paradiso, who sends you to Paradise?

Yes.

How come?

Filomena slept at hers, because Mara didn't want to be alone in the house.

And so?

Nothing, I hadn't realised Mara and Filomena were such good friends.

Do you mean *friends* friends?

No, Luigi, I don't mean anything, it was just weird seeing them together, and then where did Filomena sleep? In bed with Mara, on the side where Vittoria's body was a few hours before?

Ah, hang on.

What?

I bumped into Tommaso coming back from the station, he says there's too much traffic and he goes to the hospital in Formia by train.

And?

He says he went to Vittoria and Mara's before they closed the coffin, and he noticed a yellowish tinge on Vittoria's face, under the make-up. He lifted one eyelid and found the sclera was yellow, and he couldn't explain the excess of bilirubin, he hadn't noticed it during the autopsy. Her heart was fine.

What tests did Tommaso do?

Drowning, water in the lungs.

Theory?

She passed out, the water was too hot, her blood pressure went down, for example. An accident.

Luigi, explain something to me. Someone who's studied

medicine for years, only to write in the report that it was an accident? I know Tommaso's a friend of yours, but still.

I'm just telling you, Lea, because it's as if Vittoria was the first person to die ever.

But did he at least go to Sandro's office and ask whether Vittoria had any illnesses?

Well, the strange thing is that Vittoria didn't have a doctor in Scauri. She wasn't one of Sandro's patients, nor Giuseppe's, and from what Tommaso found out from asking around, their colleagues in Formia and Gaeta weren't treating her either.

And where did she go to get her prescriptions?

Perhaps she didn't need anyone, she worked in the pharmacy after all.

But she must have had a doctor.

But not here.

They must be in Rome. But how can we find Vittoria's doctor among all the others in Rome?

Perhaps Mara knows, but why do you have to find them, Le'?

Something doesn't add up for me, and now this yellowish colour. Why doesn't Tommaso ask for further tests?

Why should he, what reason is there? You seem to be the only one who can't accept Vittoria's death.

I don't think so, since Tommaso went around asking who Vittoria's doctor was.

Why are you making that face?

Look, did Tommaso really do the autopsy?

I gave Luigi a look full of hate, which I occasionally did. He was so opinionated when he spoke, with that irritatingly confident expression and that tone of someone who's studied physics. They know everything. As if everything can be explained and understood. When we argued, he would laugh, which made me even angrier, and say, Why are you so insecure, this is the way I talk, why do you get offended? There was no reason at all why I should be offended; however I was very well aware that without him I would be a freer woman, I would travel more. He, on the other hand, despite his studies, his communist faith, his Party friends, his great political passion and practice, was a tribal leader. His tribe was me and the girls. Also, the only women he considered intelligent, although he blabbed on about how there was no difference between males and females, were his daughters. Because he had made them. Little Athenas born directly from his own thigh. Luigi was unbearable, but he was a good-looking man and his looks soothed me, or at least they had until now. Or perhaps I was just in love with him full stop. You can judge people by their friends but not by who they love, absolutely not, but I judged myself on everything. Loves, fears, what I didn't understand and could have. I judged myself for my vices, badly. After all, I locked myself in the bathroom to smoke.

Vittoria hadn't been living in Scauri long when Councillor Comi got married. He was a member of the town council at the time. We stood shoulder to shoulder outside the Immacolata ready to throw rice. She whispered She said yes by chance, and because she was in a good mood.

Why had I said yes to Luigi? Why had she said yes to Avvocato Pontecorvo? Do you die by accident and get married because you're in a good mood?

Putting it all in line, one phrase after another, the Vittoria issue was this. A woman dies in the bathtub, by drowning. The medical examiner finds water in her lungs and does not investigate further, although he knows, like everyone else, that the woman is an excellent swimmer. Perhaps the medical examiner doesn't perform an autopsy, we don't know why. The woman is over sixty. At the funeral, the town she lived in for the last twenty years senses that she was more than she seemed. On the contrary: perhaps not at all what she seemed. But what did she seem? The woman had a husband she hadn't seen for over ten years. The woman was a doctor but didn't practise, she worked in a pharmacy. Four days after her death, the medical examiner reveals to an ex-schoolmate that he noticed a yellowish tinge to her complexion and checked that the whites of the eyes were also yellow. The woman who drowned in the tub did not have a doctor in Scauri. She probably had one in Rome, where she was born, where she lived for the first forty years of her life, where she studied and spent her married life, where Rebecca probably lives, the friend to whom she left a sculpted Sibyl head. A Canova plaster. Rebecca's surname is Lanza. The woman who owned a Canova plaster, a museum piece. Which, along with the gloves and clothes of the people who came from Rome to the funeral, indicated affluence, perhaps even wealth, contrary to appearances. And which we might have imagined, given that as soon as she came to town she bought a house and then, a few years later, a boat. All in cash. Scauri and Rome are only a hundred and forty kilometres apart, yet these misunderstandings, this lack of knowledge, this lazy assumption so as not to bother asking, or taking for granted instead of explaining, are so huge that Scauri and Rome might be on different continents. Oceans apart. We know more about our relatives who emigrated to Argentina or Canadà – pronounced with an accent, French-style – than about this woman who died in her bath. Two streets away from our house. Drowned. It must be said that relatives from Argentina are very interested in talking about themselves, perhaps also out of boastfulness, while the deceased woman had no interest in talking about herself. On the contrary, as her husband reiterated, her first instinct was to say nothing. It may be that economic class, or social class, separates people more than geography. Money is more divisive than oceans. To take that point further, one might say that the only difference in a species, our own, that has no races, is social class. Money more than skin colour, more than sexual orientation, more than religious belief. One last thing. The woman who died in the tub lived the last twenty years, and shared her bed, with a much younger woman who could have been her daughter, and who knew her husband. There was no love lost between the two of them, in fact they hated each other. This young woman, who could accurately be defined as her widow, like the husband, has made friends – when and why is unknown as yet – with a woman almost the same age, originally from

Scauri, who works in the funeral parlour and, since the death of the drowned woman, could and may have benefited financially. Who your friends are tells us who you are. You can be judged by your friends.

Why don't you say something, Lea?
 I'm thinking about what you said.
 And what did I say?
 That I'm the only one interested in Vittoria's death, but that's not true, otherwise you wouldn't have told me that thing about Tommaso and the yellow.
 Because I know you're interested.
 Lui', listen to me. I am and always have been interested in things that are unclear to me, and Vittoria's death is unclear, and I owe myself this at least.
 You owe it to yourself?
 Yes, I don't understand anything about this woman.
 If she wanted you to understand something, she'd have told you, Lea, but instead she was okay with it.
 And then her husband, the attentive Avvocato Pontecorvo, told me to stay out of it, but he seemed threatening, and so.
 You read too much Tex Willer, my love, and you watch loads of films.
 I finished my wine, and wondered what Luigi would do if I died in those same circumstances.

I liked Tex Willer. He had his own idea of justice, and so did I. Silvia and Giulia liked him too. At first they just looked at the pictures, and then they gradually started reading it. They often asked for a steak two fingers thick. And a heap of chips. I went to smoke a cigarette in the bathroom but it was a mild evening, so I went down into the garden and then kept walking. First the pathway that crossed my mother-in-law's brothers' vegetable plots, then Via Olivella, and then, one cigarette after another, along the direct Rome-to-Naples railway, where trains ran continuously. I found myself in Via Romanelli, in front of Vittoria's house. The lights were on in Constantinople, bathing the patio in gold. The garden was in full autumn bloom. Cyclamen and chrysanthemums, the huge pinky-white bellflowers almost as high as the carport now. The pink acacia flowers were so bright the tree looked like a powder puff. The box and the willow displayed all the extremes of all shades of green. The nettles. A flickering light came from the kitchen, like candlelight, and some music I didn't recognise. Unsure whether to go in or not, I lit another cigarette. So when Filomena opened the door to let Sibilla into the garden, and leave a bucket of vegetable peelings outside, she found me standing there, in front of the gate. At least I was holding a cigarette.

Lea? What are you doing?

Nothing, looking at the Constantinople tree.

Do you want to come in?

Are you inviting me into someone else's house?

This has always been an open house.

*

Cabbage leaves in the bucket. Yet another shade of green. Mara stood in front of a mirror in her petticoat, a glass of grappa on the dresser, pinning her braids around her head. She smiled at me without turning around. I saw her reflection, the same Mara as ever, not the woman who had sat in my office and listened to the reading of a will that concerned her. I was convinced Mara had already known all about the will. And so had Filomena. I sat looking at my distorted image in the glass tabletop. I looked away and watched Filomena go over to the little table next to the mirror where Mara was arranging her hair, pick up the glass of grappa, drink a sip, and then come back to sit with me. I couldn't hold back.

Where were you on Sunday morning?

And you, Lea? Where were you?

I was in Ponza, with Luigi, at my friend Alba's house.

Did you have a good Sunday, Le'?

Quite good. What did you do?

I was in the office.

On a Sunday?

Yes, you're not the only one who works, I have stuff to do too.

Who could possibly think you have nothing to do. Were you alone?

I don't make enough money to pay for a secretary.

On the other hand, Filomena, my mum and dad didn't pass their drudgery on to me.

They did, Le', but you didn't fancy working the land, you wanted to be married to a teacher, didn't you? With daughters who do well in school, with their shiny Primigi shoes, and weekends in your friends' houses.

Sibilla had flopped down on the rug in front of the unlit fireplace, the cats were sleeping in the pewter bowl in front of me, from somewhere I could hear cheeping, like chicks, and the scratching of paws on a wooden door.

What's going on?

The canaries on the terrace, the cages are out there, there wasn't room in the garden. Come on, I'll show you.

Mara took me by the hand. Filomena stayed sitting where she was. She picked up the packet of cigarettes I'd left on the table and lit one.

I didn't know you smoked.

You don't know a lot of things, Le'.

Mara yanked my arm. Come on.

There were two rectangular chicken coops on the roof terrace with canaries, parakeets, and a very colourful parrot inside. I had been expecting birdcages.

A parrot? Whose is it?

Councillor Comi's. He went on holiday to Brazil with his wife and kids two years ago, to see relatives.

I think I knew that.

They came back crazy about parrots. They bought this one in Naples, but nobody warned them it would grow so big.

And so?

Nothing, you know what people are like with animals, they get tired of them.

What's the parrot called?

Giacomo.

What a name for a parrot.

The younger daughter, Mariella, you know who I mean?

Yes, maybe.

Well, Mariella took her school-leaving exam and despite not studying at all for five years apparently she had some enlightenment about a Leopardi poem, I can't remember which one now, the Councillor did tell me.

I left my cigarettes downstairs.

You see why Vittoria liked talking to you? You'd remember the Giacomo Leopardi poem, you might even know it by heart. Which poem could it be?

The Village Saturday Night? To Silvia? The Infinite?

It was about birds.

The Lonely Sparrow?

No, no sparrows, a dead swallow and a man who comes home on a cart, and he dies too.

But that's not Leopardi, it's The Tenth of August.

Yes, The Tenth of August! And who's it by?

Giovanni Pascoli.

I told you Mariella never studied in five years of secondary school. What do I do now, change the parrot's name?

We burst out laughing, squawking Giovanni, Giovanni at the parrot, which wasn't particularly upset. After a minute it started repeating Giovanni, Giovanni in a croaky voice that reminded me of Uncle Alvise, Filippo's uncle who had lived with his sister-in-law after his brother died. Uncle Alvise was nice, I was sorry when he died. No one knows what goes on in other people's houses, never mind in other people's beds.

Mara, is that an owl too?

Where?

There, outside the cage.

No, it's Gallina Nera, he spends his time croaking at the birds he can't catch, or perhaps he's trying to talk to us.

Filomena appeared with the pack of cigarettes and offered me one as if they were hers. I took it, she lit it for me, then she did the same with Mara. Leaning on a low wall we smoked, watching the birds, which were gradually quietening down. Perhaps Filomena was a cuckoo, entering other people's nests and chasing out the rightful owners.

The following morning I went back to the ironmonger's. I talked to Riccardo, made him tell me his version. I hadn't found an opportunity to do that, and during the night I had scolded myself for it. His parents stayed to listen.

I said to him, You're blonde like a girl, and he threw a bottle at me, at my face, I dodged it and went to punch him, I was looking stupid in front of my mates, and anyway they come here and think they can take our girls off us.

Girls will decide for themselves.

No, money decides, these guys've got more money, and they smell of perfume like gays even if they aren't.

Why do you say things like that?

I don't want to disrespect you, Le', but you're a woman even if you're a lawyer.

What's that got to do with— Never mind, keep going.

I went over and punched him, it's a lie that I missed, he moved a bit, but I reckon I broke his cheekbone.

You did not break his cheekbone.

You reckon they'd tell you? Did you see him at the funeral? His face was all swollen up.

No, his face wasn't swollen up.

Anyway, I was getting ready to punch him again and he headbutted me and smashed my nose, then the others held me back else he'd never have got up off the ground.

All right, you came off worst.

I'm telling you, three of them were holding me back else I'd have smashed his face in.

His mother laid a hand on his shoulder and his father, coughing, asked him to watch his language, in a feeble voice. Neither the gesture nor the reproach made any difference.

Vittoria called me an idiot.

Vittoria?

Yeah, Vittoria, she appeared out of nowhere, like a demon. She said You idiot, you'll get your parents in trouble.

And then?

I said Shut up, dyke.

How dare you?

What, she's not a dyke? And how dare she speak to me like that in front of my mates and those rich kids from Rome. Then she reached over and touched my face and all, I thought she was going to hit me. I don't hit women ever, not even ones that are bitches or those ones who don't know their place, so I shut my eyes and I thought a slap from her wouldn't hurt anyway, and instead she fixed my nose.

What do you mean?

She took my nose, squeezed it hard, pulled and moved it, I don't know, something clicked and it almost stopped bleeding. Then she went over to the other guy, checked if he was okay, and then left. She called me an idiot again, and if she wasn't a woman I'd have hit her, but I don't hit women. When my nose stopped bleeding I thought it was beautiful though, Le', it was sunset, it was all yellow and orange, like a disco. Funny, isn't it, someone Grandma's age at a disco?

In the office, I tried to get over the bad mood the conversation with Riccardo had put me in, and thought about Rebecca Lanza, who would receive a Canova head as a gift. I felt stupid. Was Rebecca the mutual friend who had told Pontecorvo? And how friendly was she with Vittoria? If I wanted to know anything, I had to ask Mara, so I picked up the phone, preparing myself for the possibility that Filomena might answer.

Mara?

Lea.

How's the head business going?

Filomena went to the post office this morning. Rebecca said she couldn't come and get it, I don't think she wanted to, I don't even know why Vittoria wanted her to have it so badly.

Was it you that told her?

No, I don't know her, I told Brigida.

And who's Brigida?

The wife of an old friend of mine who also knew Avvocato Pontecorvo. He's called Carlo, he's nothing to do with it, forget it. Are you coming round later to get something to remember her by?

Like what?

A jumper, a ring, whatever you want.

Aren't you worried the plaster head might get broken?

I've never cared about that head, I could have smashed it myself, but Vittoria loved it, it's one of the few things she brought from Rome.

Was it a gift from someone? A family treasure? Something like that?

I don't know, Lea, but if I'd broken it before the will was read, it wouldn't have been my fault, would it?

No, of course not.

It's one of the few things she brought with her when she left her husband's house.

I see. And is Rebecca a relative?

I don't think I've ever seen her. I told you, she was a friend. They met at boarding school. Vittoria went to two boarding schools, but not in Switzerland, in Rome, on the Via Cassia. I lived in Via Cassia as well, after Isola Farnese, but no boarding schools for me, it was the countryside. I was scared walking home at night, the road was dark, but the air was good and my dad and mum weren't the sort who ask questions.

What questions?

Like how I brought money home. I had three brothers and my mum didn't work.

You had brothers?

They're all dead, everyone dies in the end, even Vittoria. Anyway, there are things to laugh about, in fact more things to laugh about than cry about. You'll have to come and get something before all our friends take everything, the De Filippis, the Nocellas, the De Stasios, the Montis.

Keep me a jumper.

Which one?

One you don't want.

You choose one and then we'll see if I want it. Giovanni, Giovanni, that was so funny last night with the parrot.

So funny, madonna. Mara, what did Vittoria mean by that sentence for Pontecorvo?

How should I know? Come on, doesn't it make you laugh thinking about the parrot with the wrong name?

And she hung up, laughing.

In the rectory, Father Michele was sitting among the children in a circle. He was talking about spinach, describing the leaves. Vittoria used to organise foraging excursions to collect wild plants in the area as far as the Redeemer. She started after a group of boys and girls got poisoned at a barbecue to celebrate the approaching school-leaving exam. They had organised a bonfire on the beach one hundred days before.

Scauri seafront is full of oleander plants. Mainly pink, but also white, and a couple of crimson ones. They're old, branchy, tough, their leaves like a mass of spears in battle, or so Luigi would tell the girls when we went for a Sunday afternoon walk. Since the pavement had been widened and some merry-go-rounds set up, they were more willing to go. Anyway, the teenagers, who had bought chickens and sausages to roast, had used oleander branches as skewers, out of laziness, convenience, or bad luck. Oleanders are beautiful but poisonous, and therefore out of fifty kids, over thirty were poisoned. Suspicion fell on the sausages, the home-made canned vegetables; drugs which mowed down the populations of both Scauri and Formia, like a spectre; mushrooms, obviously, because they'd eaten those too, finding them who knew where, since in May there aren't many to be picked around our way. And then Vittoria came out with the story of the skewers.

We did all know that oleander was poisonous, but we thought it was the flowers and leaves, never the branches.

All parts of the oleander are poisonous, Vittoria had said, in that way of speaking she had: without judging but leaving no possibility of redemption either. It's almost always impossible to correct people. But one thing compensates another. And with a bit of luck, this can be like correction. So she went to Father Michele, who had only been there a few months at that point and was also from Rome – not exactly Rome, but Guidonia or Tivoli. I'm from the bottom of the Tiburtina, he would say, confident that even if they didn't know where the Tiburtina was, everyone would have heard of it at least once.

It was a short step from the wild herb collection campaigns to herbaria. Scauri wasn't a rich place, and those herbaria cost less than sticker albums. Manuela from the stationer's wasn't happy, and nor was the newsagent, because sales of Panini albums and stickers dropped.

The children liked them – poisonous plants were included – and the families liked them, because they saved money and felt part of a bigger world outside their back gardens. And I think Vittoria had fun, children didn't bore her.

When Germano, Scauri's old and perhaps first stationmaster and Vittoria's bridge partner, died last year, Vittoria said to me on the way out of the church You know, it's sad that the people who welcomed me when I first came here are dying. I didn't have the courage to tell her that Germano was a diehard fascist, although she might have simply answered with a shrug: Who cares.

Vittoria did more for Scauri than Scauri did for Vittoria. The town didn't acknowledge this fact, but I did, and perhaps this was why I wanted to find out more about her death. It was obvious that everyone was grateful to Vittoria, and loved her, but I liked to tell myself that I was more grateful. Avvocato Pontecorvo had called it fever. However, immersed in that feeling of gratitude, with the smell of incense crawling out of the church and winding its way into nostrils and thoughts, I watched Father Michele talking to the children about spinach leaves, how not to confuse them with mandrake, which could be toxic, and showing them the differences between aubergine leaves and belladonna, and a thought made its way into my mind that had nothing to do with the sense of community but a lot to do with money. But how.

As if he were aware of that nagging thought, perhaps disturbed by the noise, Father Michele smiled at me. Our dear Vittoria, God rest her soul, these herbaria are beautiful, aren't they, children? All the herbs and flowers in our area, all the leaves season by season, and even aquatic plants, seaweed and salicornia, they're beautiful. They're beautiful, repeated the children, in clear voices that didn't, however, manage to erase the questions crowding my brain. Money buys money, and human beings buy human beings? Was that the point? Even my own thoughts weren't clear.

I was ungrateful. Scauri knew very well who Vittoria was, and also that Vittoria had given the town more than she had received in return. But Scauri was sure it had no need to thank her because it had welcomed her in spite of the fact that she lived outside the established rules of nature, which Vittoria had demonstrated she knew well. She knew earthly plants better than heavenly ones, by her own admission.

When the children came out two by two, saying goodbye to Father Michele happily and waving their hands, I sat down on a little chair. I sat in silence, my knees on a level with my face. I wrapped my arms round them. Father Michele was quiet too.

Have you been to the cemetery, Lea?

You know I don't like cemeteries, and the dead are dead and the living are living.

I went and planted the herbs, the ones I managed to find at Patella's.

How is Patella? I haven't seen him for ages.

A bit run-down, Lea, but well. Anyway, even though capers are difficult and have minds of their own, Patella says they grow well up there at the cemetery, so I put two chiapparielli caper plants on the grave.

I don't think there are any capers at the boneyard, Father Miche'.

There were, but on the old columbaria.

The ones that collapsed.

Yes, then I planted rosemary, sage, lavender – which goes well with rosemary – thyme, normal and lemon, marjoram, and hot chilli peppers. What else could go there?

I don't know, parsley and basil are seasonal. Lemon balm perhaps?

That's not a bad idea, you're right. Shall we go to my room? You look uncomfortable there.

No, I like it here.

Tell me, Lea, why didn't you become a teacher?

It never crossed my mind, and I might not have been very good at it. Look at Luigi, he doesn't get upset when the students don't know something they should know, he laughs it off and explains again, with different words or examples. You need a lot of patience, which I don't have, not even with Silvia and Giulia. I do their homework with them and straight away I'm wondering, why don't they know this already?

Do you know the answer, Lea?

Basically, no one knows anything, but if you make the effort, you learn.

I think so too, but I'm not a teacher, I'm a priest. I don't teach, I hear confession and absolve, it's different.

Did Vittoria confess?

Occasionally. Not real confessions, in the sense that we never talked in the confessional, only ever in my room, or here, or sometimes behind the altar when I was putting away the wafers in the tabernacle. But she never asked me to absolve her, and in any case she never talked about sins.

If you're telling me this, it means you don't need to keep that professional confidentiality rule of yours in this case.

No, I don't, but I've thought back over Vittoria's words many times in the last few days and I don't think there's anything to add to what we knew, that is, she had a husband, and left him in Rome when she moved here to live with Mara.

But did you know she was a doctor?

I did know, of course. She was a very good doctor. I consulted her on many occasions for myself and also occasionally for parishioners who couldn't go to other doctors.

How do you mean?

Sensitive matters – you know everything is a delicate balance in this town.

Father Michele, I have to tell you something.

I'm listening, my child.

There are things I don't understand.

Tell me, Lea.

Why did we never know she was married?

She didn't see fit to tell us.

Didn't you know?

No, she never told me.

Did you ever ask her?

No, I never asked if she was married. By the way, how did the bottle case turn out?

With a financial settlement. The Romans will pay Riccardo and his parents fifteen million to keep it quiet. They don't want their young man to have a criminal record. As Pontecorvo took pains to underline, he has more opportunities than Riccardo, and they don't want it known that he broke someone's nose one autumn day.

They're generous, they left a considerable donation after the service, although the funeral was paid for.

Who by?

By Vittoria. When she gave me the envelope with her will, she also gave me the money for the funeral service.

And what did you say?

That it seemed premature, that if she needed to tell me something I was there, and anyway it wasn't necessary, with everything she did for the parish, and all the money she gave us, it really wasn't necessary. But Vittoria just laughed and said Take this money and do what you want with it. If you don't need it for my funeral, there will be plenty of opportunities to make better use of it.

And then?

Then she went off with that walk of hers. I miss it, I must admit. Yesterday, I went into the pharmacy and realised she was dead when I didn't see her behind the counter.

But there's eternal life, Father Michele, religion should be a comfort, this is only a vale of tears.

Why do you talk like that, Lea? Don't let sorrow cloud the tenderness of your gaze. I don't think Vittoria knew she was going to die, I've already told you, I think there comes a time when you want to be sure your affairs are in order. Religion tells me that the eternal life exists, and so does the resurrection of the body, but I know these bodies are immobile and confused in God's light. Or perhaps not immobile, swaying. But Vittoria's steps, her walk, that way she had of laughing, opening her eyes wide, turning in surprise, holding her head in three-quarter profile, focusing on something then huffing slightly, they're things of this life and no other, of this world and no other, and I'll always miss her way of walking.

But Father Michele, I think Vittoria did know she was dying, and didn't tell anyone.

Why not?

That's the question we need to answer.

Why do you think that?

Because she gave me the will, and therefore, consciously or subconsciously, she wanted me to know her story.

Vittoria wasn't one for explanations, Lea. If you understood, you understood, if you didn't, no problem. We may well not understand, we don't always pretend not to understand: it's possible to genuinely not understand, my child.

At home, the girls were playing. I was half an hour late. With a slight air of reproach, Paola grabbed her coat, kissed Giulia's head, and left, making it clear that the next day she would not arrive at eight but at half past. I've always found reprisals tiresome. Perhaps I studied the law to prove to myself that the tiresomeness of point against point was human, if not healthy, that trial by ordeal, the fastest kind of trial imaginable, has nothing to do with justice, and nor does an eye for an eye, a tooth for a tooth. I sat down and asked Giulia who her Barbies were. I could hear Silvia messing about with water in the bathroom, humming a wedding march. She must be really focused, she hadn't answered my Hello darling, and didn't even look out when Paola slammed the door as if we had quarrelled. In a prim little voice, Giulia began a preposterous story about people lost in the rainforest. Again.

They had overturned the chairs and fixed my scarves with rubber bands between the four wooden legs. The Barbies lived in makeshift stilt houses. The encampment of overturned chairs and scarves was the work of Silvia, who was more interested in structures than human beings. Luigi was convinced she would be an engineer, which I don't think he was particularly keen on, because he had studied physics and considered engineers to be surveyors with a degree. How that piece of paper, the degree, makes you feel superior to everyone else, I've never been able to explain, but perhaps it's because I didn't study physics. Giulia said the Barbies were lost in the jungle, but they would survive because they had studied palaeobotany – she used that word but I wasn't surprised, the posters of *Jurassic Park* eyed us from walls and metal billboards, even where it was not allowed – anthropology and physics. None of my daughters' Barbies studied law or had a lawyer's office. Barbies were scientists, they studied physics. Obviously physicist Barbie always solved problems more quickly than the others and saved everyone. Where did I go wrong?

While Giulia was telling me how they had found shelter in the trees and escaped attack from first a velociraptor and then a gorilla (Luigi had read them *Congo*, and since *The X-Files* had just started I knew that sooner or later the Barbies would escape an alien abduction too), Silvia came back into the room, hiding something behind her back. She blushed when she saw me. What's up? I asked her, in the gentlest tone I could muster, but she stopped and looked left and right as if seeking an escape route. I stood and she backed up to the wall. Gently but firmly, I put my hands behind her back and felt a Barbie trapped in her fingers. I tried to take it, but she resisted. I smiled at her, knelt down, and asked why she was hiding it. Silvia fixed her eyes on the floor and burst into tears. I hugged her but couldn't calm her down. As often happened, Giulia started crying too, so when Luigi came back he found two overturned chairs covered in scarves, a woman still in her coat and shoulder bag kneeling down, and two grizzling girls. The premise for a tragedy.

Luigi hardly ever lost his temper and now, sure enough, he took off his coat, put down his bag, and said a cheerful So what's happening? Has the time come to buy the Barbie house?

The Barbie house, the cars and horses and Kens, were a recurring theme. All our daughters' friends had the Barbie accessories and they didn't. Which meant they could go and play in their friends' homes but the friends couldn't come equipped with their Barbies to play at ours. Not having so much as a Barbie camper was an unbearable disgrace. Though unable to name it, they could have described the feeling of shame perfectly, and that is what they felt. They felt poor. They didn't even have Barbie clothes, apart from what the doll had been wearing in the packaging it came in, and this, I supposed, was the reason why the settings of their adventures were all a bit wild and epic, because they dressed them in tunics they made from offcuts of their grandma's fabrics. That creativity of theirs made me love them very much.

One day, Silvia had asked me Mamma, are we poor?

Luigi's question about the Barbie house had led me to hope that we might move to another house far away from my mother-in-law. Perhaps Barbies really were an opportunity for emancipation.

Luigi opened up his arms and said to Silvia Come here, my darling. And Silvia, one hand behind her back and the other drying her tears, went between his knees, resting her head on his chest. Daddy, she sighed.

So what's going on?

Silvia showed the Barbie. Don't be angry, Mamma. I cut her hair.

Giulia stole the short-haired Barbie and made her climb up on the chair, imitating rock climbing with kitchen twine as rope, which I didn't notice at first, and made her kiss the long-haired Barbie, who was lying on a mattress of oven gloves. Then she gave a radiant smile and informed us, We have Ken. The short-haired Barbie is a man.

At Lo Scoglio, Tommaso was alone at what I considered my table. I waved at him and without even saying hello to Tobia, I went over.

Can I sit down a minute?

He was drinking a red beer. I asked for one too, although it wasn't even five o'clock.

Tomma', what's the deal with the yellow sclera?

No one in the family asked anything, Lea, not even Mara. After all, Vittoria wasn't a young girl. But when I went to see Mara at the house I noticed that, despite the make-up, Vittoria's skin was yellowish.

I went as well but I didn't notice, or perhaps I did, but it looked more bluish.

All right, Lea, but I notice stuff.

And what could it be?

Yellow sclera, high bilirubin.

Which means?

A lot of things, including pancreatic cancer.

Sorry, Tomma', didn't you notice that when you did the autopsy?

The police asked me to check whether or not she drowned and – I swear, I feel like a fraud – I just checked whether there was water in the lungs, and there was, so when her head went under she was still breathing but unconscious. I feel like an idiot now.

You can act like an idiot but not be one. Then what?

And then I didn't want to ruin Vittoria.

What do you mean?

I didn't want to disfigure her body.

Tell me something, Tomma', do you think Vittoria was ill?

What I think, Lea, is that I've only seen yellow sclera like that in the terminal stages of pancreatic cancer. But she drowned, she didn't die of cancer, if that's what she had.

But did you perform an autopsy?

What can I say, Lea?

What can you say? Never mind. But how did she end up so yellow two days later?

Nothing strange about that. What's strange is that I didn't find any medicines in the cabinet, and Mara claims Vittoria wasn't taking any. In fact she didn't see a single GP in the whole of the gulf.

Perhaps Vittoria's doctor was somewhere else. The pharmacist says she often went to Rome.

That doesn't make sense, why would someone have their GP somewhere else?

Does it sound to you like anything you're saying makes sense, Tomma'? You said you didn't want to disfigure her body, can you hear yourself? Didn't Filomena say anything?

No, she says she looked like other old people she's dressed and made up before putting them in the coffin.

Do you think we could ask to exhume the body and carry out a proper examination?

Lea, I told you something in confidence, and anyway, there's no reason to examine her again, she drowned, I know that much.

I need to understand.

You know better than I do how these things go, and anyway, neither you nor I can ask for the autopsy to be repeated, and neither can Mara.

No, she'd have to ask the husband. But why didn't you do the whole thing?

For Christ's sake, Lea, I told you, I couldn't do a proper post-mortem examination because I felt bad.

But what did you feel bad about?

I've always liked Vittoria, since I was boy.

How do you mean?

I liked her, she was beautiful, she smelt nice, she smiled, she moved elegantly. Perhaps she reminded me of my mum.

Tomma', can you hear yourself?

What can I say? I remember the exact day I saw her for the first time. I was sitting in Piazza Rotelli, I was back from university. I was with Antonio from Tremensuoli and Nino, you remember them, don't you?

And?

Nothing. I see this woman cutting across the square, staring at the pine trees, and while she's walking she takes off her sunglasses and puts one arm in her mouth, she looks up at the pines again, then she smiles at someone and looks down, and raises her hand to wave hello to them. She stares at the facade of the church and shrugs. She must have been thinking it was a dump, like everyone does, well, like we do. And when she reaches the bench she stops and looks at us, looks at me, I think she was looking right at me, and then she walks on.

What's this about?

Wait, then she comes back and says to me, That's a nice bag, young man. But who called you "young man" in Scauri? If anything, they said "son", and in any case if an older person spoke to you, they used your name. My dad gave me that bag, he gave me his own bag, this one I still use.

And then?

Then nothing, I remember her perfume and her skirt, the way it moved around her knees like a sort of vortex. She was like a pizzica dancer. If you watched her skirt moving, it was like she was dancing the pizzica. I remember hearing castanets too.

So you didn't do the post-mortem because of those knees twenty years ago?

Mara was at home, alone. The glass in front of her looked like the same one from the night before. As well as the ginger cat in the pewter bowl, Gallina Nera was there, licking his fur. Mara was slurring.

Filomena has nothing to do with all this, leave her alone, you know what she's like.

No, what's she like?

A simple person who likes me, and I like people who like me, only them, and that's mainly why I liked Vittoria. Maybe I can tell you how we met.

I only came by to get a jumper.

That's not true, you ask a lot of questions, about Rebecca too, and about Avvocato Pontecorvo, and me, and Filomena, and the new cats. You don't think Vittoria died by accident, which can happen. I didn't kill her, I wasn't home, ask the gas bottle guy who gave me a lift.

No, I don't think she died by accident, and I don't think you killed her, but why are you all so fixated on this accident theory?

Stop it, please, go and get a jumper, they're in the right-hand side of the wardrobe, mine are on the left, take those too if you want, I've had enough of staying here with all this stuff. Stuff turns you into stuff.

The bedroom was dim, the bed unmade. It looked like two people had slept in it. I pulled up the shutter and the noise startled the birds on the terrace. A fluttering of wings and shrill calls followed, and it sounded to me like they were entwined round the pipes holding up the carport roof along with those pinkish bellflowers that were blooming late. They would wilt and we would see them again in spring. Not Vittoria, though, not any of us.

Would Vittorio want that old wooden boat when he was eighteen? It went so slowly and made a noise like a coffee-pot, and keeping it up was like an Eastern spiritual exercise. Vittoria's perfume was fading in the room, despite the little bottles of essential oils still there on the dresser. It still lingered in the wardrobe, though. I took two deep breaths and opened my eyes wide. I stretched out a hand and took a coffee-coloured polo neck with a fabric pin still attached to it, one I'd seen her wear often. White threads of her hair gleamed on it. I opened a drawer of socks, looked at them, unmatched and untidy. I sat down and started sorting them. Blue with blue, grey with grey, striped with striped, white with white. There were pants and bras too. I looked incredulously at the bits of fabric. Furtively I slipped a pair of lacy, very transparent flesh-coloured pants into my pocket. Whose were they? It's odd to wonder about ownership of objects when you're in someone else's house and those objects are certainly theirs. It's odd to trust your own idea of the world when you only need to look. There were very many socks. I couldn't tell the black from the blue any more, and that held me up so long that Mara decided to join me. She was swaying on her feet, even though she was leaning against one door of the wardrobe.

Have you been drinking since last night?

What am I supposed to do?

I don't know.

Of course you don't, Lea.

Tell me then.

No, I'm tired now, but I'll talk to you. Perhaps it's good for me to tell someone something. Wait, don't just take a jumper, take some trousers, they don't fit me, or they'd be too short for me, but you wear boots, you can tuck them inside. They're nice trousers, warm, she'd be happy you took them. She liked you.

Stop it, Mara, it's not true.

It is, though, she liked you. I don't know if she liked you that way, I hope not, and if so I hope I never find out.

I'm not like you two.

How would you know what I'm like?

I like men.

But you liked Vittoria too.

Yes, I did.

So how many women do you have to like before you say you like women?

But only in theory. I didn't like her the way I like Luigi.

Why didn't you ever try it?

It never occurred to me, and I'm not a homewrecker.

But who says you would have managed to wreck us? And how would you know what wrecks a home anyway?

And you do know?

Of course I do. Just one thing.

Which is?

The inability to accept that those we love change.

I left Mara's house with a pile of trousers, and thought that autumn and winter would pass and I would wear them. The act of putting on and taking off those trousers would mark out the days. The last milk teeth placed under pillows for the tooth fairy would be transformed into coins, the pages of the physics textbook Luigi was writing would pile up on the kitchen dresser to be revised and corrected. Riccardo, the ironmonger's son, would have fifteen million lire. Pontecorvo's nephew would forget he ever threw a bottle. The herbs on Vittoria's grave would grow and fill the cemetery air with the scent of sage, thyme, and rosemary. I also thought about how, under those trousers, heavy or light, Vittoria had been naked. And now I was too. Naked in the same place, but not at the same time.

At home, I asked Paola to help me with my wardrobe change, I had delayed it. More than anything, I wanted to make room for the trousers. This procedure amused the girls, who tried on dresses, jackets, and shirts, ties, and hats. Necklaces and hats sent them into raptures, who knows why. Sometimes they would weave peacock feathers together to make tiaras or circlets with such gusto, I didn't know where it came from – perhaps books about gods and heroes. The feathers had been a gift from Vittoria for Giulia's christening. Their vivid colours had faded but they were still beautiful. I would be sorry to have to throw them away at some point, but I was even more sorry to deny the girls something they enjoyed. Perhaps the feathers had had their day. They didn't have Barbie clothes but they could play at being Barbies with my and Luigi's clothes.

Mamma, are we poor?

I gave Paola some shirts and trousers, knowing they'd be tight on her but that she, like many other women at that time, was good at little dressmaking jobs. My mother-in-law, an accomplished seamstress, disagreed. She treated Paola with scorn, and snorted when Luigi insisted that her darning was very good. She protested that she hadn't given him an education to then go around dressed like a tramp.

I believe you when you talk about scientific things and medicines, but you have to believe me when I talk about my work, it's not what you do but how you do things, my mother-in-law would protest.

Some of the trousers I remembered Vittoria wearing, others I was sure I had never seen before. Some had patches on the bum, the same sort you put on elbows, and the repairs were generally visible, a fabric version of that Japanese practice of mending with gold. At first I had thought it a wonderful idea and metaphor, but since everyone had started using it to mean anything and took more and more liberties, I had taken a dislike to it. While I was placing the patched pair of trousers on the hanger, I heard jingling, a five-hundred-lire coin, and Silvia, a great collector of current coins, hurried to pick it up. Smiling, I put my hands in the pockets.

Silvia ran around me excitedly chanting More coins! More coins! But all I found in the pockets was a broken toothpick and a train ticket from four weeks before. One of those new one-day distance-based tickets valid on all the routes in the Lazio region. The band on the acid-green, or perhaps mint-green, card stated that on 9 September, the day after the town festival, Vittoria had bought a one-day ticket in the 160-kilometre bracket. That is, she had been to Rome and back.

The stamp was faded but I managed to read it. She had left on the seven o'clock train and returned on the five o'clock one. From Tiburtina station. I held up the ticket to show the girls the watermark – I did it with banknotes as well, when the mint issued new denominations – and along with those circles and squares that opened a parallel space between two sheets of paper, I glimpsed some writing on the back. It was the same handwriting as the will. *D. Via Tagliamento 12.*

I exchanged the five hundred lire in my own pocket with the one that had fallen out of Vittoria's, now hot from my daughter's damp, greedy palm, and went into the room I used as a study, though it was actually a storeroom on the balcony, freezing in winter and boiling in summer. I arranged the three items in a line and looked at them. Like a rebus. A five-hundred-lire coin. Half a toothpick. A kilometric train ticket. The letter for the rebus was D. Unable to solve it, I stared at the items. Then the phone rang, causing me to reconsider an idea I had discarded.

Pursued by the ringing phone, I went out into the street with no curiosity about who might be calling at that time of the afternoon, and what they might have to say to Luigi or me. It might be parents of the girls' classmates or the classmates themselves, who were thoroughly familiar with the telephone at the age of ten. I reached the Via Appia and continued walking briskly. It was almost sunset and the sky was pink. Outside Il Passeggero restaurant there was the usual aroma of the wood oven. Two waiters were standing there smoking, and I said hello: one, Giovanni, had been in my class at primary school. I had a sudden feeling, and turned. On the other side of the road was the funeral parlour, Paradiso. Filomena was standing in the doorway, looking at me. Another rebus. Hairdresser's – funeral parlour – butcher's – household goods. This was the set-up. Unsure what to do, I raised my hand to wave. She didn't respond and I kept walking. And I also kept walking when Anna, Riccardo's mum, came towards me, brushing her off with a haste that was unlike me and that even I found vulgar. I'll ring you tomorrow, I said with a smile, in an attempt to excuse myself, and finally I entered the newsagent's.

I crossed the first room, grabbed the two phone directories for Rome, and went out again, apologising and promising to bring them back the next morning. I must have looked so determined that Aldo, the newsagent, stopped with his cigarette halfway to his mouth, his hazel eyes behind dark lenses, and all he said was Eh, but that might have been involuntary, a spasm, a comment on the ash that dusted the glossy newspapers.

What d'you want them directories for, Le'? called a voice I didn't recognise, behind me.

In the office, I told Cristina she could go, rang Luigi to let him know I was in the office and wouldn't be back for dinner, and might be late, and started looking for telephone numbers that corresponded to 12 Via Tagliamento. The letter D might be the initial of a surname or a staircase. In Rome, flat complexes were towns. Then, with all the meticulousness I'd applied in my university years and when specialising in the state archives, I switched off the overhead light, switched on the banker's lamp I was so proud of, which towered over my desk, and started searching. I had to start somewhere, and

I was betting on the surname initial. And I also knew, with a certain annoyance, that luck is almost always worth more than accuracy.

One hour later I had learned that there was no block of flats at number 12 Via Tagliamento. There was Paolo Dini, Ulisse Dini, Duccio Maria Dini, next to whose name was the specification MEDICAL PRACTICE. I had an excuse to go there: Avvocato Pontecorvo. I rang Cristina at home and asked her to tell him I would stop by in the late afternoon the next day, to settle the bottle case.

But it's Saturday, he might be busy.

He won't be.

Father Michele was sitting under the little roof that sheltered platforms two and three, waiting for the train. He was wearing a black overcoat and his country curate's hat with a wide round brim, the one for special occasions, and his usual trainers. When he saw me, his face broke into a smile, which I returned, happily.

Where are you going, Father?

To the Vatican.

To do what?

Nothing in particular, I'm going to pick up the rosaries for our parishioners.

All the way to the Vatican?

There's no need, Lea, but once or perhaps twice a year I take the trip. I like that ciborium, the columns, the facade, and all the people who come from a world I will never see. It's an outing, basically, does that surprise you?

No, I'm thinking of the church door with that annual balance stuck on it, where the parishioners, who are also citizens, can check how much comes in from the curia and the cost of services.

Few christenings, funerals mostly, my dear Lea, but thank goodness for that, death brings the community together.

Not all deaths, Father Michele, some are desertions or tragic accidents, as they say here.

Look, Vittoria had lived her life. You'll say Gisella's death was a tragedy, but Vittoria's wasn't, it was something that could happen, like it could happen to me.

I don't think it happened to Vittoria.

What are you talking about, Lea? Anyway, tell me, where are you off to?

I'm going to Rome too, to settle the ironmonger's son's case. I'm going to get the cheque and sign a document that says Riccardo and his parents will have no further claims. I think I will have to sign a confidentiality agreement.

I've never understood the need for these documents myself. Writing something down can't cancel out what happened or prevent it from happening again, it's not magic, is it?

Father Michele, this from you, who say the words Body-of-Christ three times a day in the certainty that the consecrated wafer is literally Christ's body?

I'm sorry I wasn't here when you were doing catechism, imagine the fun we'd have had.

Do you think so, Father?

I do, I do, I always have fun with children. Suffer the little children to come to me, as it's written.

Is the train late?

I don't think so. Listen to me, Lea. Do you remember

when you came over yesterday, or the day before, when I was talking about the spinach leaves?

Yes, of course.

Well, my dear, such a coincidence. A little girl from Sessa, Alice, who often comes to play in the oratory because her grandparents are here in Scauri, brought me a bag of spinach as a gift. You know, I always get chickens, rabbits, vegetables, occasionally eggs, and even, I must add, cheeses, like ricotta, which I love to eat for breakfast on toast, with jam, they bring me jam too. Anyway, never mind breakfast, let's always be thankful for those who bring these gifts so I can share them with those more in need than myself, and I don't have much. Anyway, I thanked Alice and took the spinach into the kitchen, and since Antonietta was still there to give me a hand, I asked her to clean it for me, so I could eat it that evening. Antonietta doesn't know how to clean a fish but she's very patient with vegetables. While I was talking to the children about palms in the Bible and the flowers Adam and Eve name in the Garden of Eden, Antonietta came into the room and said, Father Miche', ring Alice's grandparents, because there's some devil's leaves mixed in with the spinach.

Devil's leaves?

You can imagine the children's reaction, Lea, half of them crying, half howling, and some in both halves jumping up and down with excitement. Devil, devil, they were shouting. So after I calmed everything down, and rang Alice's grandparents, I set about explaining the difference between spinach and mandrake. You arrived shortly after.

The whistle of the train interrupted Father Michele's monologue, and I wondered if I'd be able to recognise a mandrake leaf, or mandrake itself. I stood up.

Please excuse me, Father, but I'm going to sit in the front carriage because I'm in a hurry, and it's quite empty until Cisterna, so I can study the documents.

I've shocked you, haven't I, Lea? he said, smiling at me, under that round brim that seemed massive compared to his face, and waved goodbye, whispering Go on, go on, and turning at once to start talking to a man and woman I knew to be from Minturno but didn't know personally.

The train braked sharply at Latina. I opened my eyes and realised I'd been asleep. I looked out of the window somewhat anxiously and saw Alba getting off and looking around, furtively. She didn't move forward or back, she was looking for someone in the crowd. When the train had already whistled, a girl came running up to Alba like a mad thing and gave her a string bag containing a perforated box. Alba handed her an envelope and got back on the train without saying goodbye. The doors closed and the carriages started moving, creating the illusion that the scenery was rushing past. Silvia and Giulia always looked forward to this moment of confusion enthusiastically. As I had thought she would, Alba came to sit in the front carriage. We always sat in the first four seats on the left when we travelled to Rome and the ones on the right on our way back to Formia, where Alba lived, so on the way we would see Rome rising above the countryside, following the ribbons of the aqueducts, and on the way back, after Itri station, we would enjoy one of the most attractive sea views in the Sud Pontino – the Gulf of Gaeta.

There was of course a hint of local pride in all this delight in the aspects of the gulf, which no university degree or knowledge of the world could or would ever be able to dent. Alba was neither surprised nor pleased to see me.

I didn't see you get on in Formia.

I got on in a rush, it was already moving, would you believe, but they hadn't shut the doors.

And what are you going to Rome for?

Nothing in particular, only a visit.

What's in the bag?

Mamma mia, Le', why the interrogation? Tell me instead about Ponza last Saturday, we haven't caught up since then. Did you have fun?

It was good, it's always lovely to stay at your place. I'm just sorry Luigi didn't swim.

I started looking out of the window again, the drainage canals, the messy houses, the silos and chimneys of the chemical plants, the sheep. The Pontine Marshes were still crowded with sheep. I thought of the Piranesi etchings, cheap copies my mother had given me when I opened my office, poor in quality and poor in definition, but I'd had them framed and hung them in the entrance hall. Who knows why Mamma thought those etchings would be suitable for a legal office, and whether, to her mind, those grainy prints were an investment.

What are you thinking, Le'?

Remember those prints Mamma gave me when I opened the office?

Piranesi?

Yes, Piranesi. I was thinking the Roman countryside always looks like Piranesi.

In colour, though.

Alba smiled, but she was giving me a worried look.

I have to tell you something, Le'.

Tell me then.

You're so judgemental, though.

Me? Since when?

No, you are, remember that time I got drunk and threw my guts up at Clarice's party in Naples?

You made an arse of yourself.

Why? I was ill, I wasn't being an arse.

The first time they invite us to a house in Vomero with people we never even dreamt of meeting, and you get pissed as a newt and throw up on the white sofa.

I was the one who threw up, not you.

But we went together.

See what you're like? Forget it.

Come on, Alba, tell me.

Don't lecture me, though.

Hey, I can say whatever I want.

Basically, my daughter's sharing a house with two Romans who each have a cat, and she wants one too.

You went down to Latina to get a pussycat?

Are you spying on me?

Of course not, Alba, I woke up suddenly and looked out to see where we were, and anyway, have you seen what you're holding? In fact, check if it's all right, I can't hear it breathing.

It's all right, it's fine. Anyway, Carla wanted a sphinx cat, you know, those furless ones?

Horrible.

Leave it, you can't judge someone by what they love. You always say that.

Yes, but still.

I said leave it, Lea, the real issue is why this cat costs over a million lire.

Are you mad?

I found one in Latina for two hundred thousand, and now I'm taking it to her.

But why?

Because I want her to fit in, like a normal girl.

With a cat that costs a million? It's expensive being normal.

You see how judgemental you are? Everyone's normal in their own way, Le'.

Let's hope it's a real sphinx cat at least, since you paid so much less.

Occasionally I thought about the fact that my mum and dad had given me a short name because they didn't want people to shorten it, as always happens around here. And that it had been pointless.

*

I met Alba the first day of secondary school. We probably wouldn't have made friends if we hadn't been put next to each other. In the second row, to the left of the teacher's desk, under the window. I would often get distracted by watching the trains – the Vitruvio Pollione liceo overlooks the station at Formia. Written on the frontispiece is POST FATA RESURGO. Class A was the rich kids' class, the ones from the good families in Formia, the ones who would follow a profession. Engineers, lawyers, doctors, secondary school or university teachers. I ended up there because I had won the gold medal at middle school. I studied hard, I wanted to get out of there but without making it obvious. I hoped things would take me away. The gold medal got me into the liceo classico and out of the vocational teacher training school. Even my mother couldn't object to that. So I studied and read a lot to help things lead me somewhere else. If I hadn't met Luigi, I might have gone further away.

The fact remains that in the first two years of this prestigious school in Formia, I was the worst dressed. My father would say Poor yes, why dirty? I was the poorest and the neatest. I think Alba and I made friends at the beginning because Alba hadn't realised where I came from. And she didn't until the first parents' evening when my mother arrived, very clean and tidy, very elegant, she always was. An elegance that, when you looked closer, was to do with the natural taste she undeniably possessed, but first and foremost with decorum.

I watched the teachers, and my classmates, and hoped my mother wouldn't notice the smirks, the superiority, the condescension. Not that they could say much, I was top of the class. Which didn't mean I was a genius in their world – I wasn't, of course – but that my performance was the result and consequence of my social class, of the deprivations and limitations. There are things women can do today that they couldn't when I was a girl in the sixties, but there were things poor people, like I was, could do and that they can no longer do today.

Yes, that means something, Luigi would groan when we talked about it. Since we had the girls, Luigi couldn't conceive of differences between boys and girls, he took it as a personal insult. When I made him read the entry for "woman" and its synonyms in the encyclopaedia, he started crying and then went to the shed to sort out the electrics and build a cabinet. In the evening, when he came back in for dinner, he was calmer, and he had a purple thumbnail, perhaps from the hammer, he was careless.

So I wondered whether Alba, with her sphinx cat, had for the first time noticed a class difference that was not in her favour, one she'd never been made to face before. Or, on the other hand, if the strangeness was due to the fact that when we were growing up you didn't buy cats or dogs, while our daughters were starting to move through a world where you could buy and sell anything. A place where care and nurture were starting to come at a price.

I could not and would not understand it, but I think I felt sorry for Alba, sitting there with the string bag on her lap with the perforated box holding the kitten inside, and who knows what inside the kitten.

When she got pregnant at seventeen in the last few months of primo liceo, I didn't feel sorry for her at all. We were great friends by then, she'd been to my parents' house lots of times, and her daughter Carla seemed like a doll to us from the start. I think that's why she was a good mother, she didn't feel any responsibility, she just wanted to play.

What Vittoria would have said about buying and selling cats, I would never know now. Nothing, probably. She would have shrugged, laughed, mocked perhaps. Once she'd told me that her dog, Sibilla, knew at least four hundred words, that she had written them down in a notebook. I wondered where the notebook was.

Termini station swallowed up Alba and her cat, and would soon swallow up Father Michele too. I hurried to the Via Marsala side exit. I liked to have a coffee in Bar Trombetta. I liked station bars. I was used to taking trains early in the morning, and station bars are always open. There were some dodgy-looking people around Termini and the car fumes had blackened the marble. It had probably been too white at first. I didn't like things that were too white. You're so narrow-minded, Lea, Vittoria would laugh, when this kind of discussion came up. Why narrow-minded? Because you have your own idea about everything in the world.

She would certainly have laughed about the story of the million-lire cat that cost two hundred thousand.

I couldn't say now if Vittoria laughed often, or laughed with me. There is an error of judgement that is easy to make, and which I instinctively guarded against: mistaking someone whose nature is to laugh at the world for someone who laughs with you, heartily. Or with love. My theories were worthless. I was confused. Sometimes you meet those enthusiastic types who seem to be in love with everyone for the first five minutes, then they get distracted because they're not in love with this or that, or you, but with everything. Well, I had always been careful to keep things separate.

Avvocato Pontecorvo's office was in Via Sicilia, in a lovely Liberty-style building. I went round by Via Marsala, telling myself that from there I would walk as far as Piazza Fiume, and take the bus to Via Tagliamento.

I liked walking around Rome. I stood with my head high, looking up at the buildings' cornices and losing myself in the forest of aerials. I liked listening to the insults between drivers, always clever and always vulgar, watching the birds perched on the trees. It wasn't peak starling season. When it was, the only solution to walking and staying clean at the same time was to go around with an umbrella, even in full sunshine.

Layers of guano and weeds emerged from the sampietrini cobblestones or cracks in the tarmac, reporting on the parking time of the cars. Some had been parked so long that the tyres were flat. Others, that had clearly been broken into, had become shelters for homeless people. They looked like those cars in the middle of meadows or ravines, or in patches of shrubs, their windows darkened with newspapers, swaying because someone is making love inside. These cars, though, were as motionless as monuments, their windows covered with yellowed, sometimes tattered sheets. And perhaps they served the same purpose as monuments. You knew where to find them. Temporary monuments, but monuments nonetheless.

Avvocato Russo, I regret that we did not meet under the best of circumstances, but I think we can declare this business of the fight closed to our mutual satisfaction. I would also like to thank you for coming. I do have Osvaldo, it's true, but at my age moving around is challenging.

Don't mention it, Avvocato Pontecorvo, you're welcome. I had to come to Rome on other business anyway.

Are you staying overnight, Lea? If so, I would love you to be my guest.

Thank you, but I'll try to get everything done in one day. I have two little girls, I can't ask my husband to be their mother too, although he may be better suited to the role than I am.

Don't say things you don't believe.

I don't say things I don't believe.

In that case, my compliments to your husband. How long have you been together?

About twenty years, but we already knew each other.

Is he from Scauri too?

Yes, he is.

And what is so attractive about Scauri that people stay and others settle there?

To be perfectly honest, avvocato, I think it's because of a certain dishevelled elegance.

What do you mean by this very poetic phrase?

There are still very few architects and engineers so the houses, which don't comply with any planning legislation, can't be more than two floors high. As you know, few plans are granted to surveyors, so this strange slice of the Pontine seafront, squeezed between the sea and the mountains and surrounded by two promontories, is a pleasant place to live. My daughters have outstanding teachers, as did I, so we're well educated, we leave to study elsewhere, we win public exams and earn doctorates, and then we return to this crescent of sand, not too light and not too dark either, ordinary sand, like pozzolanic ash. We walk among the Roman ruins of ancient Minturnae – there's a beautiful capital there, I don't know how long it'll last – or in the English cemetery. If you get a chance to visit, the way the graves are laid out demonstrates how a colonial empire works. And we watch others, and are watched in turn.

Avvocato Pontecorvo looked at me with a hint of a smile whose benevolence I was unable to gauge. I stood up and offered him my hand.

Is that a convincing enough explanation for you to move to Scauri?

No, but I enjoy listening to you, Avvocato Russo.

May I ask you something?

It is, as you know, polite to answer.

When did you meet Mara?

At the party I told you about, in March 1972. My cousin Carlo turned up at my house with her. We had thrown a party.

Your cousin Carlo?

Yes, a man who liked very young, beautiful girls, and in those days Mara was both.

And what did Vittoria think?

I've told you that too, but I don't believe you understood me, so I wonder, Avvocato Russo, what you know about married life.

Number 12 Via Tagliamento was a little three-storey building in what might be defined as neoclassical style. The pale-yellow facade was marked out with slightly embossed white pilasters topped with flat capitals which, by the look of them, hadn't been restored in quite a while. The space between the house and the road was taken up with flagstones between which three- or perhaps four-leafed clover poked through. The real garden was probably at the back. Two square pillars stood either side of the green gate, each topped with a pine cone. On the right-hand pillar was the entryphone. Four bells. One initial of the names on each of them was D. The fourth one simply said MEDICAL PRACTICE. I rang the bell. A metallic voice said Come in, first door on the left after the front door. I looked around for reassurance and cues. I didn't know what I would say, ask, do, or demand. Who I would find. The waiting room was as I had imagined. Sober, light, with magazines on the little table. I picked up *Oggi* and started reading. What would Dr Dini look like? How old was he?

I had an idea he was a colleague of Vittoria's from her university days.

A woman came out of one of the two doors opening onto the room, not much older than I was, or perhaps she was older than me, wearing a knee-length, light-grey skirt, a pink sweater, and a pair of blue-framed glasses. Everything was pastel. Perhaps I was too, but I didn't realise.

Signora Albrigi, please come in.

I'm not Signora Albrigi, and I don't have an appointment. I wanted to speak to Dr Dini.

The doctor's no longer here, he died. There's Dr Rebecca Lanza now, we've been here just over a month.

Then I'd like to speak to Dr Lanza.

What about?

A friend of mine, Vittoria Basile.

Dr Lanza only receives by appointment.

So I imagine, but I need to speak to her, it won't take long.

Wait a moment.

I went back to reading *Oggi*, and an article about exiled royals. My heart was pounding. I was nervous, I didn't know what to expect or, if it came to it, what to say. Thus, focused on myself, it didn't occur to me that the woman who sat down beside me might not be the slightly late Signora Albrigi but the doctor herself.

Lea, I suppose.

Yes?

Rebecca Lanza, welcome.

And the head?

At my home, returned to the source.

Dr Lanza looked like my grandmother. Very much like her. She was very elegant, slimmer, younger too, but she looked like my grandmother. My father's mother, whom I resembled. In short, Dr Lanza and I looked alike. I froze on my chair. Was this the reason Vittoria liked me?

I closed my eyes and opened them again. I closed them again, and that's when the doctor's voice reached me in the dark. Don't worry, she said, then added Gianna, bring Avvocato Russo a glass of water.

Dr Lanza knew a lot more than me, and perhaps about me. Vittoria had mentioned me to her.

I've only had a coffee since this morning, that must be it.

It happens. Do you enjoy and suffer from low blood pressure?

Yes. I laughed, and so did the doctor. Then she sighed.

Vittoria was ill. She had pancreatic cancer, which she more or less diagnosed herself just over six months ago. She wouldn't hear of operations or treatment. Not that an operation guarantees a cure in this type of disease, and certainly not in Vittoria's case, but it might have lengthened her life. Vittoria was sure you'd turn up sooner or later, Lea, but I don't think she imagined it would be so soon. Perhaps it's easier to follow tracks when they're fresh.

Who else knew about Vittoria's illness?

No one.

Not even Mara?

Vittoria didn't want Mara to be made aware of it, Avvocato Russo.

Why?

She wouldn't tell me.

I don't understand.

I can't say I've ever understood much about the woman.

Do you know Mara?

I've only seen her once, and I don't think she'd remember me, nor do I think Vittoria's told her about me. Vittoria wasn't an open book.

Why wouldn't she recognise you?

It's been years, and anyway I was wearing a costume.

How do you mean?

Literally. We were at a fancy-dress party, at Vittoria and Giorgio's house. Haven't you ever been to a fancy-dress party?

There was something asymmetric about Rebecca Lanza's eyes, they were sort of misaligned, for which reason I felt enveloped in the dark-green gaze of this woman who was more or less Vittoria's age, had a Canova plaster of a Sibyl head at home, and had met Mara only once, at a costume party. Avvocato Pontecorvo had said it was a party for Vittoria's forty-third birthday.

Why did Vittoria want you to have the head?

Because it's mine, it's always belonged to the family.

And why did Vittoria have it?

It was a love token, a gift for what I believed would be our eternal bond. I'm not ashamed to talk this way, because

I suppose we all have these kinds of thoughts. I stopped thinking I was special years ago.

Vittoria kept the head when it was over between you, and you didn't ask for it back?

First of all, it was a gift, and then I imagine, though I never had the courage to ask her, that she thought of me every morning. How would you define love, avvocato, if not as the first thing you think about each morning, every morning you are alive? I certainly thought about her every day.

I don't know, doctor, I can't define love. Perhaps my daughters, I don't know.

Anyway, Vittoria let herself die, or perhaps she killed herself. I can't tell you because I didn't see the body. But she knew she was dying, and since the head has returned to the palace, as Vittoria in that rather scornful way of hers called my family's house, I suppose she put her affairs in order.

Who notified you of her death?

Brigida, the wife of Carlo, a cousin of Giorgio's, who died a few years ago. Brigida and Mara kept in touch. After all, you know what Shakespeare said?

No.

Things bad begun make strong themselves by ill.

But what happened?

I'm in two minds, avvocato. On the one hand I know I shouldn't tell you anything, because Vittoria obviously didn't tell you anything about her life, in spite of everything. And on the other, Vittoria did not expressly ask me not to talk about it, so I feel authorised to do so. But not here and now, I'm expecting two patients, I'm still a doctor.

Do you think Vittoria might have taken her own life?

I'm almost certain she did, but obviously, as I told you, I have no proof.

But why?

I think because of Mara, but to answer that I'd really have to think about it, and I don't want to.

Did she drown herself in the bath?

Are you joking? Drowning yourself, choking yourself, is extremely difficult. Vittoria's always loved poisons. Don't make that face. She loved cumin, too, for example, it's a fantastic disinfectant for the intestine, which is why it's so widely used in the East. It's useful for your hands too, try it, you'll have orange palms. Very chic, Vittoria used to say.

Sitting on the little stone bench next to the steps leading to number 12 Via Tagliamento, I looked at the weeds between the flagstones to convince myself they actually were clover, smaller than the leaves the girls would pick in the fields and place in their herbarium. Vittoria would probably have known the name of this species, or variety. Or perhaps not, perhaps Vittoria was interested in poisonous herbs and plants and berries for another reason, perhaps she had thought her whole life about poisoning herself. Perhaps she had already tried and it hadn't worked. Suicide attempts can fail. I waited for Dr Lanza and thought about how many times I had bumped into Vittoria with bags of herbs, coming and going from above the slope, or the sea, or Monte d'Oro. I never thought she might be interested in manufacturing poisons. If manufacture is the right verb. She made medicines, after all.

The phone booth on the other side of the road made me think of Silvia, Giulia, and Luigi. Of those of us who had lived alongside a woman who could have killed us as she cured us. The difference between drugs and poisons. Proportion. I found a few coins in my pocket and dialled my home number. At that time all three should be home. Paola answered. Luigi and the girls had gone out for a walk. The Prof had an appointment and "took them girlies with him".

Where did they go?

What, Le', am I going to ask your husband where he spends his time? He's a teacher.

Wanna Marchi lookalike Paola's veneration for Luigi was ridiculous. Or rather, not for him, for his title. I'd heard her saying to the greengrocer, or at the supermarket, The Prof likes this, The Prof doesn't like that, although I was the one who paid her wages and I had hired her because, between physics and the Party, Luigi didn't have time. So those feelings of respect didn't depend on the job – they'd have been the same or greater if Luigi had been a lawyer, or a doctor – but on sex. Paola showed respect to men and didn't trust women, myself included. Bearers of guilt, bearers of pain and penises. I wondered whether my daughters would have to grow up as I had, in a world that not only accepted this order of ideas but considered it unalterable. To Paola, I was unnatural, violating a social order, just as I was to Filomena and many people in town who had loved Vittoria without judgement simply because she came from outside and was a pharmacist. They probably wouldn't have allowed a female doctor to treat them, unless she was a gynaecologist.

Take care, Pa', see you tomorrow.

Bye, Le', what's the weather like in Rome, chilly is it?

Like in Scauri.

Eh, but as soon as you go north a bit it gets colder.

I returned to the little stone bench, said goodbye to the two women who had been examined by Dr Lanza, and saw the secretary come out. She gave me a respectful half-smile. I smoked, waiting for the doctor to emerge.

Oh, wonderful! Will you give me a cigarette? I've finished mine.

I held out the packet to her but she stopped me.

Please, please light it and pass it to me, I need to find my car keys.

I found myself putting the cigarette between my lips, holding my bag between my knees, and fumbling with the matches. When Rebecca finally extracted her car keys from her bag, she turned, jubilant. Then, stretching out a hand and never taking her eyes from mine, she took the cigarette from my lips and put it between her own. I heard a thud. The bag I was holding between my knees had fallen down.

Let's go, avvocato, I still have a lot to tell you.

I haven't got long, I have a train to catch.

It's not a simple story, and I'm not sure how much I'll be able to tell you. Don't rush me.

But I.

Do you want to know the story or not? That's my car.

When I found myself putting the events of that day in order, which happened more than once during the days to follow, I would start by deciding how it started, that is, with me being gobsmacked because I had never seen a car like Rebecca Lanza's. Not one woman who was not a close friend of mine – so only Alba, perhaps Marisa – had ever gone so far as to put a hand up to my mouth, remove the cigarette from my lips, and start smoking it. This stranger had. I wondered how Marisa was, I hadn't heard from her for days. I wondered if Carla had liked the cat or realised it was a fake.

Perhaps Rebecca was seducing the girl in the past who I reminded her of.

Perhaps she was thinking of Vittoria, me and Vittoria.

I don't know. Anyway, the car was a black Alfa Romeo Duetto, very shiny, with lemon-yellow seats.

Do you prefer wine or a cocktail? Don't tell me you don't drink.

No, no, I do, I drink.

So wine or cocktail?

Don't rush me, doctor, I answered, smiling.

I opened the car door without realising that the convertible, the umbrella pines transforming the sky into an archipelago of pale-blue puddles, the sound of the wheels on the cobblestones like popcorn jumping, the memory of Vittoria's perfume between Dr Lanza's fingers as she took the cigarette from my lips, making me long for something that had never happened and never would – all these things taken together and one by one had made me fall into the trap I was starting to glimpse in this story, that is, that care and seduction show themselves in the same way. Drug and poison.

The sharp braking shook me.
Where are we?
At the Locarno, Vittoria used to like it.
What?
The hotel and bar. You know, there weren't many places in Rome after the war, in the mid-forties, where they would rent a room to two girls. Of course, it was more difficult for men. Besides, we had that air of being from a good family that wards off suspicion, although I always went around dressed the same as I am now, you see.
Your clothes look normal to me.
I felt observed, first by the man at the door and then by the one in reception, then by two maids, who scuttled into a service corridor, and lastly by the bartender, who asked, without even looking up, A Martini for you, and for your friend? A gin and tonic, I heard myself answer. Any preference for the gin? asked the man behind the counter, sanctioning my outsider status with the question. Beefeater red, said Rebecca, confidently.
As I was telling you, we used to come here because we liked to stay at Rosati in the square until late, and because it

reminded us of Paris. We'd been to Paris for three months in the summer of '46 and that's where we fell in love. I certainly fell in love with Vittoria, but I don't imagine she ever talked to you about me.

She didn't talk to me about anyone.

I wondered whether the image of that unknown girl sitting at Bar Rosati in the forties would resemble the woman I had known: how, and how much? Above all, I wondered if the woman Rebecca was talking about with an ease I wouldn't have believed possible for people who had lived that type of life – outside a system of rights and duties, excluded from rights above all – if that woman was dead, or whether I had yet to meet her. Whether she was about to appear, step out of the door, enter the garden, sit under the leafless pergola, perhaps a wisteria, take a seat on a white cushion placed there to soften the iron chairs and backrests, and say to me, simply, Have you got a light? Would she order a Kir, or was Kir linked to Scauri too? I also quickly learned that Vittoria had in fact smoked her whole life and still did, although I had never seen her do it.

Do you think Vittoria was acting a part in Scauri?

I don't understand the question, avvocato. Vittoria is exactly the woman you knew.

No, Dr Lanza, I don't think so. The woman I knew wasn't a witch who manufactured poisons to kill herself with.

Oh please, poisons and drugs have the same ingredients, it depends on the quantities.

Yes, but.

Yes, but what? A woman, a doctor, an excellent doctor who knows she has no hope, doesn't she have the right to save herself and those around her from all the suffering she's decided she is unable to bear? Shouldn't we all have that right?

She never struck me as a woman who would kill herself. She had loads of friends, she was respected in Scauri, loved, I would say.

Avvocato Russo, life is bigger than Scauri, surely you'll grant me that.

So you both graduated in medicine.

Yes, Vittoria a year earlier, with better marks. She went straight to America. She said I'm going to America, as if she'd said I'm going to Ostia, to L'Antica Pineta. Have you ever been there? Excellent restaurant. Anyway, I asked her When are you coming back? She kissed me and said Soon, you concentrate on getting your degree. I felt like a child.

And did she come back soon?

Three years later. She had married Giorgio in Mexico.

But didn't they get married in London?

That's what Giorgio always says. Mexico seemed too poor a place to him, unpredictable, ambiguous, too sunny as well.

And how did you take it?

I went to dinner when she invited me, to introduce her husband to me.

What happened?

Nothing, what was going to happen? Giorgio knew everything, I suppose, and I suppose he didn't mind.

What are you trying to tell me?

Nothing, avvocato, I've got no reason to skirt the issue. Vittoria is the woman I loved in my youth, and if it wasn't pathetic I would tell you I still love her. But she's dead, and I'm taking the opportunity to talk about her with you because you saw her often in the last twenty years. In fact, I'm expecting you to tell me something I don't know, so I can delude myself for a moment that Vittoria is still alive, deceive this old brain that there's still time, although I know that if I'm lucky I have more alcohol than time, and that's not so bad. I said Giorgio didn't mind, as far as I learned in the following years, until Mara came along.

What is it that Avvocato Pontecorvo didn't mind?

I know you've met him. Don't worry, I'm not spying on you. It's through Brigida again, she told me about a row in which the heir apparent of the house Pontecorvo d'Aquino played the lead. I tend to digress, forgive me. He didn't mind that his wife liked women, it excited him. After all, like me and many others, he was in love with Vittoria, the way she moved like a wild animal, or a cat, always on tiptoes, sly, camouflaged like a jaguar and as much of a predator as him, fluttering like a butterfly as well.

And so?

So you would go to a party at their house dressed one way and come out dressed another. Or naked.

And Vittoria?

Vittoria what? What are you asking? The queen of the party. We were young, it was really fun, AIDS was far in the future. I went home naked in a Cinquecento at least twice. One morning, it was so late, or so early, I didn't manage to stop off at the palace, I was on call at the hospital. So I got to the ward naked, going in the back door though, obviously, and I ordered the two nurses I met to get me a white coat because someone had stolen my clothes on the beach at Fregene. After that I became the doctor who swam naked. They were fun years. I still am the doctor who swims naked. Funny, isn't it?

I've never been swimming naked.

What? Lea! We'll have to make up for it. Anyway, Vittoria liked the sea too, very much, she always liked it. You might not know this, avvocato, but Vittoria's maternal grandmother was Venetian. Vittoria spent the war years in Pellestrina, it was a safe place.

I've never been there, dottoressa. I've been to Venice once, after I left school, but the centre of Venice, San Marco, you know, Rialto Bridge, all that.

Anyway, Pellestrina is a strip of sand and tamarisk that doesn't even offer any shade, and not a lot else. A few bell towers, a lot of lagoon. Vittoria would go with her grandmother. I think it's still like that, a place with no beach resorts, wild, a few rocks, wooden huts left on the beach by the sea, stone slabs placed there to protect La Serenissima, fishermen, old, fortified islets, perhaps used as armouries. You could eat cheaply, drink even more cheaply, the doors of the churches were open, the same surnames heard again and again from the voices from the street. She showed me photos. Vittoria as a girl was the same, same face, that lovely nose. Anyway, I went there once with her, she was happy, jumping the waves. Once she jumped so much she lost her costume, tits out. She used to wear those bandeau ones without tying it round her neck. In the end we took off our bikinis, we were young, there was no one on the beach. When we came to Scauri for the first time, over forty years ago, she said it reminded her of her childhood beach. How the Tyrrhenian coast could remind her of the northern Adriatic, I don't know. But you know, feelings are what remind us of things, almost exclusively feelings. I preferred the Sassolini beach, but then I do prefer rocks. You should go to Pellestrina, just once, trust me.

Rebecca, forgive me for going back to those parties, but – why did you use to go?

I had fun. And I had no other way to be with Vittoria, touch her, kiss her. She didn't want to see me alone, and I think it also annoyed her, in some way I've never been able to understand, that I went to live with the woman I still live with now. I don't think she was jealous, it was ownership, a lazy ownership, but Vittoria was possessive.

And do you love her?

Elisabetta? Of course I love her, how do you stay for nearly forty years with someone you don't love?

A sense of obligation?

Perhaps, yes, that's possible, but as far as I'm concerned I know I'm too old to love someone else for forty years, because I'm not forty years old. Even if I fell in love with her now, went for all my check-ups and lived a life of self-discipline, how many more years do I have ahead of me, ten? Ten good years, hopefully? Eight good, two less good? I'd choose to leave the way Vittoria did.

Which way is that?

Dying when it's still possible to seduce someone and be sure that someone will miss us for a while, that they'll still look for us even when we no longer care to find ourselves. It makes me so happy, Lea, and in the end I'm not surprised that at over sixty years of age Vittoria succeeded in something that's impossible for most people.

What?

Being the object of honest curiosity.

Are you saying you went to bed with Giorgio, too?

Yes, many times, but I don't remember anything about it. Giorgio, Carlo, Filippo, who remembers now? Does it matter? No, I do remember one thing.

What's that, if I may ask?

The first time I only took my pants off.

And Vittoria?

She bent to kiss me and asked me why I hadn't brought Elisabetta.

And why hadn't you?

Elisabetta was never interested in that type of thing.

Didn't it bother her that you were?

We've never been conventional people, and not communists or moralists either.

Why do you think it bothered Vittoria that you lived with someone?

I believe she thought I would never have asked her to live with me because of my family.

What about your family?

Drink up, avvocato, your gin and tonic's getting warm.

It's not warm out.

No, it's not, but have a sip, don't make me get drunk alone. Light me another cigarette.

Do you have to look for more keys?

I don't like lighting cigarettes. I don't like peeling mandarins or oranges either, that first sour taste of peel.

In that case.

Vittoria always used to say that.

Her husband said it.

It's an expression of hers. Don't use it, it's not a nice one.

Why not?

Think about it.

Later, Dr Lanza, let's go back to your family.

Well, Vittoria thought they were too aristocratic to allow me the rash decision of living with a woman, but they weren't. She never understood the aristocracy, she liked artists, scientists, the sacred breed, in short. She thought the wealthy were almost all idiots. I should add, though, that my mother didn't like Vittoria, but she wasn't homophobic, as they say now, or no more than anyone else, she just didn't like Vittoria, only she couldn't say so. It wasn't the norm socially or culturally, you decide which, to talk about a woman as another woman's girlfriend. With my boyfriends she was always fierce. Would you like another gin and tonic?

No, not right now, I'll have a cigarette. So where does Mara come in?

Pastimes can very easily become vices, Avvocato Russo. At a certain point, Avvocato Pontecorvo no longer had enough friends, and at that point, I think it might have been 1972, Vittoria would have given it up too. She would shortly take the public exam to be a full professor, a female professor in a faculty of men. Never mind honour killings, gay marriage, and adoption for single mothers, there was talk of a real revolution, never mind '68. Vittoria was a radical feminist, that job broke down the gates of an ancient castle, set a precedent, in other words. I think Vittoria knew that. I think that despite her tendency to downplay everything, she realised it was important, not that she had to vindicate anything. She didn't like categories, she liked artists or scientists perhaps. As I was saying, Vittoria came from a family of professionals who had never had access to the academic world. Those famous horrific racial laws. They weren't on the right side of history, and institutions have a long memory, at least the ones who call themselves total institutions do, and I include universities in those, ours in particular. Anyway, one evening, the evening I saw Mara, I was dressed as a musketeer, with a pair of socks down my pants to make everything look like what it was meant to be.

Which musketeer?

Athos.

No one ever chooses him.

As I was saying, few people understand the aristocracy. Anyway, this very young girl turned up at the fancy-dress party, she looked a lot younger than she was, dressed like a white bellflower, beautiful, Mara was truly beautiful. I haven't seen her since, but she was charming, and that charm disturbed me, and I think Vittoria too, and many other women present, dressed as women or as men, with or without socks padding out their pants. It had nothing to do with seduction but with touching and immediately after protecting. Picking, to stay with the flower idea. I can't really explain, it's as though in the end purity must be violated. It was strange, and also because Mara had never been anything else in her life.

Apart from?

A tart, Avvocato Russo. Until she met Vittoria, Mara engaged in prostitution, as they used to say. I'm not judging her for it, to be clear, everyone can do whatever they choose with their body. But that evening Giorgio was very drunk and very enchanted, as we all were, believe me, by this slender, voluptuous, white bellflower. A devil's trumpet, speaking of poisonous plants. And although she put up some resistance because she wanted to dance – you know how it is, we all want to dance – Giorgio grabbed hold of her as if picking a flower, tore her from the liana the flower had climbed up, and shut himself in the bedroom with her. I think Mara wanted to be picked, but she also wanted to be able to say stop. Carlo, Giorgio's beloved cousin with whom Mara had come, tried forcing the door, knocking, but to no avail. We heard her scream, then cry, then Giorgio came out leaving the door open behind him, and three or four of us ran in. Mara's clothes were ripped and she was in a corner holding a piece of Limoges porcelain, a girl holding a basket of flowers. That's something else I've never forgotten. A pile of banknotes on the bedside table. Vittoria took care of her all these years. Vittoria takes care of others, not vice versa.

The first train from Roma Termini station in the morning goes to Scauri-Minturno. I'd only taken it once when I went with my brother to Venice and then Florence, after my school-leaving exam. We spent some of the night on the wooden benches at Santa Maria Novella and took an overnight intercity, possibly without tickets, or perhaps with tickets but without paying the fast train supplement. We got to Termini at about four. I haven't seen many stations, but I find Termini beautiful. Anyway, it doesn't matter how many things you've seen, how many people you've loved, how many children you've been lucky enough to have or not have, not everything is comparative.

When the fast train stopped at platform twelve or thirteen, the coveted central platforms, at four o'clock that morning, as the city awoke, if it had ever been to sleep, I saw the marble sides as white as teeth among those strange brown cavities or fillings in the Minerva Medica temple along Via Giolitti, and Porta Maggiore and the little towers and buildings around, from whose balconies the sight of the liquid iron maze of those tracks could puzzle you or even drive you mad; that morning Termini and I fell in love. I think it was mutual, because nothing ever happened to me there and the love never ended.

So as I waited, drunk on Rebecca's words even more than the gin and tonic, for the last train to Scauri, I told myself I had nothing to fear and that there was no need to ring Luigi and risk the phone waking the girls.

I was counting on being home by one, and I'd tell him everything.

Though I didn't know what everything was, I might understand by telling him.

The first time I took the girls to Rome, we went to Vatican City. On the way in, Silvia made the sign of the cross. Giulia was little and I think in the phase when the most exciting thing to explore was her own nose.

When we went to Florence the following year, to see Luigi's very nice uncle and aunt, Silvia asked me why Santa Maria Novella station wasn't called Termini, since the tracks finished there. I'd never asked myself that, and not even Luigi had a theory, which rarely happened. It was easy to imagine that the name was geographical in nature, as often happened with stations. But Silvia, believing in her brainwave, went on telling everyone she had been to Firenze Termini on the train.

A few years later I brought up this anecdote with Vittoria. I met her at the station, when one of us was coming back from Rome. She was wearing a strange quilted coat with a strange furry lining, a sort of Barbour. Only grey.

The Barbour's lining, also known as dead dog, was a vital element of the shepherds' costume in the live nativity scene in church on Christmas night. It made Luigi laugh because it's usually the richest families whose children, with their cerulean-blue eyes and blonde curls, get the roles of angels or Jesus, Joseph, and Mary. But in Scauri, where the well-off families were the only ones equipped with those prestigious English jackets, they were shepherds.

Vittoria's Barbour was longer, like a hunter's or fisherman's coat. In answer to a question about the girls, I told her about Firenze Termini and she said of course, my theory was correct, Termini is a locative possessive: delle Terme, of the spas. After the Baths of Diocletian, just outside the station. And they're beautiful too, the spaces are. If you've never been, go.

I was thinking how I would always have liked to suggest a trip to Vittoria, or for her to suggest it to me. It did happen once, she invited me out on the boat, but we never actually went. Perhaps planning is pointless, perhaps planning creates an obligation that immediately becomes emotional, or like work. Planning takes away lightness, and to me Vittoria had always seemed capable of saying Go, not Let's go. Or perhaps, I thought, now I knew about her husband, the parties, Rebecca, Mara herself, Vittoria had used that "we" so many times that she no longer wanted to.

We'd had afternoons and mornings, a few coffees and a few lunches, and not even one night.

What would have happened at night.

With no delays, the train arrived at Scauri on platform two. You had to cross platform one to leave the station, there was no underpass or overpass. Only the train conductor and I got off. We both looked left and right when we crossed. The train would leave again the next morning. The conductor and I exchanged silent nods, I think, of goodnight. My car was sleeping in the square outside the station. It was an emerald-green Seat Ibiza. The light was still on at the railwaymen's club, but it was hardly the time to go and knock now, and perhaps the light wasn't a sign of someone's presence but rather their forgetfulness.

There will always be a light on for you in this room, I prayed for Vittoria, without knowing whether I would be able to keep that promise, at least to myself.

Luigi welcomed me home with a row. Silent and mimed, because Silvia and Giulia were asleep. It started because when I came in I blew him a kiss and signalled to him that I'd be right back, and hurried into the girls' room. I opened the door and looked at my daughters. Silvia was sleeping on her front, completely covered with the sheet and blanket. Giulia was sleeping like a bug overturned on its carapace, arms raised and outspread. I was overwhelmed with a dark tenderness, the awareness that I would never again be alone in life and the anxiety that at some point, hopefully, they would be left alone. Alone without me. Before I could close the door, Luigi pulled my sleeve, signalled me to keep quiet, and dragged me into the living room.

What are you doing?

What time do you call this? Where have you been?

Working, what's wrong with you?

Until one in the morning?

I was in Rome.

Why didn't you let me know?

I rang you in the afternoon. Ask your beloved Paola, you were out with the girls on some errand of yours.

I was home at seven putting dinner on the table.

If I threw back in your face all the times I put dinner on the table.

What's that got to do with it, you're.

I'm what? Don't say it, all right, studies, open-mindedness, gossip, and then you tell me it's my job because I'm a woman and a mother?

Don't start playing the victim now, or worse still the feminist, you've come home at almost one in the morning and you smell of gin.

What, you're checking on me now?

Is asking checking?

In that threatening tone, and dragging me in here?

Are you going to take me to court, avvocato?

Why are you kicking up all this fuss now?

Because I'm your husband and I want to know where the fuck you've been for a whole day without telling me anything. Even housemates let each other know, for God's sake.

I went to settle the Riccardo business, remember the fight with the ironmonger's son? All right, you only give a shit about your stuff, but it's not even been a week.

A whole day to sign a document?

No, not only that.

What else then?

He sat down with his legs spread and his arms crossed, he looked furious. I wanted to laugh. And it annoyed me too, a pouting child of forty-two. I went into the kitchen, opened a can of beer and started drinking it. I liked beer. Without getting up, Luigi grumbled in a tone that might have been put on and might have been real resentment, Aren't you going to bring your husband a beer?

So I got another, opened it, and when I reached the sofa I poured it over his head. He yelled. I gestured to him to be quiet, the girls were sleeping. I was laughing like a hyena. Do hyenas laugh? He tried to slap me, but I dodged and kicked him back onto the sofa. A gentle kick. He sprang back up, grabbed my arm, lifted me, and pushed me against the wall. I kept kicking at him and he kept squeezing, we looked at each other with hate.

How we went from fury to laughter, I don't know. Love, or sixth sense, the ridiculous, saved us once again. The sense of, or instinct for, the ridiculous.

I wonder, Avvocato Russo, what you know about married life. You'll agree with me that the world is larger than Scauri.

Will you let go of me now?

Are you going to tell me what you did?

I found a train ticket in a pair of Vittoria's trousers, the ones Mara gave me.

So?

There was an address, and I went there.

But why?
She killed herself, Lui'.
What are you talking about?
Vittoria killed herself.
Why?
She was ill.
And who knew about it?
No one.
Who told you this?
The doctor who was sort of treating her.
The one whose address it was?
Yes, she's also the Rebecca from the will. Coincidences don't exist.
Why do you smell of gin though?
She took me for a drink in a beautiful hotel, the Locarno, near Piazza del Popolo.
Posh people's stuff.
We're in a world of posh people, Luigi, we didn't realise it but Vittoria was a lady. I realised, but I thought it was a spiritual thing.
Not only.
It has nothing do with wealth, though.
No, of course not, Lea, but.
The strangest part is that Rebecca looks like me, or rather, I look like her.
What's that got to do with it?
Maybe that we always like the same things. Go and dry off otherwise you'll catch cold with your hair wet with beer.

Standing in front of the bathroom mirror wearing the lace pants that might have been Vittoria's, I smoked and couldn't look myself in the eye. I'd dreamt about palm trees that night. But not the ones on the seafront at Scauri, not much taller than the oleanders and definitely less flourishing. Desert palms. An oasis like in films or a puzzle magazine. I watched the palm fruits fall, they looked like gold nuggets. They fell on me, leaving a golden froth on my skin without a bump or pain. I closed my eyes and enjoyed this unexpected warm rain. In the distance, cotton plants. Perhaps I was near the Nile. Distracted by a sound, I looked away and saw Vittoria, sitting on the bank of a watering hole, pouring water from a jug. I went over and asked Why? Vittoria smiled, put down the jug, took my face in her hands, kissed me. I closed my eyes again. In the dream I was happy. Another noise, a voice, two voices. I pulled my lips away from Vittoria's and looked round. My daughters were running towards me, turning round often, as if something or someone was chasing them. I smiled a goodbye at Vittoria, blushing, and started walking. After a while I fell, I got up again, I tripped, the girls ran towards me without reaching me, I couldn't reach them either. The third time I fell I realised I had a rubber lace round my foot, tied with two little silver links. The bracelet Vittoria was buried with came out of the ground and tied me to it.

Restless on Sunday morning, while everyone was still asleep, I started preparing chicken broth. I always kept a chicken in the freezer. I peeled the carrots, removed the celery leaves, crushed the garlic, added ginger root and Parmesan rind from which I had grated off the wax, two juniper berries, and a few cumin seeds. I peeled an onion and tears came to my eyes. I cried. When I had stuck cloves into the onions, Silvia came in, pillow creases marking her face, eyes half closed, and hugged me. I raised my hands, which smelt of onion, and bent to kiss her head. She smelt like Johnson's Baby. Happily, I lit the stove, washed my hands, and picked her up. She snuggled between my shoulder and neck to go back to sleep. I heard Giulia's scurrying little footsteps, then she appeared and climbed up to stand on a chair and hug both me and her sister. I was happy. I put my nose in Giulia's hair and smelt milk.

Come on, sit down and I'll get your breakfast.

Around the table, still covered in vegetable peelings and spices, Silvia and Giulia started playing with the cloves. Giulia sneezed and Silvia said Now I'll cure you, like Vittoria taught me.

I turned, in sudden panic.

Vittoria cured colds with cloves?

Yes, Mamma. You have to take a clove and put it on a lit match. The top of the clove pops like a popcorn. Then you hold the stalk of the clove, put it in water, count to seven, and drink two sips. And then your temperature and cold will get better.

Come on, Mamma, let's try! cheered Giulia, sneezing.

I filled a glass with water, lit the little gas ring, took a clove, and held it over the flame. The top of the clove popped like popcorn. I threw the stalk in the glass, counted to seven, and told Giulia to drink. Giulia drank. Silvia continued using the packet of cloves as a maraca and Luigi, coming into the kitchen, said happily Mulled wine for breakfast?

Papà, papà, we're curing Giulia's cold like Vittoria showed us.

Luigi looked at me, then at the ceiling. First your parents with the pendulum, now the posh lady's spells. I can't be doing with superstition, Le'.

Although the ironmonger and his wife seemed satisfied, and Riccardo behaved more politely than the last time, I left the shop with the feeling that something was still unresolved. It was a cool morning, still early, and there was already something unresolved.

I was confused because, when I went in, I smelt coffee, milk, and biscuits in thick bedroom air. I knew they lived upstairs, that the door to the right of the counter led to the stairs up to the house, but that sudden family smell in a business open to the public disgusted me. I felt as out of place as those smells. They thanked me and asked for my bill. I told them I'd get my secretary to send them the details, and advised Riccardo to be careful, telling him I hoped the money would allow him to get to university more easily, and with less commuting, than I had had to do. I and many others. The fashion for getting a place in Naples or Rome had just begun in Scauri. And brought with it, as the story of Alba's daughter Carla proved, other optional extras, to use a car salesman's term. Such as a sphinx cat.

I wondered what my daughters would study, if they did study, if they would ask to rent a room, and where, or whether they would express a wish to study somewhere else, abroad. Luigi and I still had a few years to think about it.

Or maybe thinking was no use, I should just get on with it.

My feet didn't stop in front of my office. They kept going to Piazza Rotelli, which was seething with the gossip of the early-morning pensioners and where the church women were lined up, getting ready to go in and torment Father Michele with requests for small loans, blessings, month's minds or perpetual Masses, mentions of deceased relatives, and more gossip, which Father Michele, who nurtured a certain taste for other people's business, did however listen to, devotedly. Luigi and I had liked Father Michele straight away because, as soon as he came, he pinned up the parish balance sheet not on the noticeboard but on the church door, and we all learned that the priest was paid about one thousand, one hundred lire per soul. We could see how much the donations and expenses added up to, how much the parish spent on organising pilgrimages and activities for children, the number and cost of funerals, christenings, and weddings.

It amused Luigi because he said that statistics originated in church records.

Father Michele was a true statist communist, so Luigi, who hadn't wanted to get married in church, had now found some motivation to please our parents, who wanted us to walk down the aisle. My mother didn't believe any other type of marriage existed, nor did my father. I've never understood what Luigi's parents think, but I imagine they'd have reacted even worse to the news of a registry office wedding.

Luigi's parents were better off than mine. They didn't work the land but belonged – though not entirely and not personally, especially my father-in-law – to that upper or lower, petty or enlightened bourgeoisie whose class consciousness consists in knowing that everything can be bought and that generally, with a few sacrifices, one can partake in the merry-go-round that transforms life into money. Above all, that one can pay in instalments and take out mortgages. Walking and imagining, I arrived in front of the railway station ready to blow up the capitalist system. But once again, I wouldn't do it.

I looked at the white building opposite the station, where there was a restaurant called Paradiso on the roof terrace. Summer and winter, the tables at Paradiso were under a pergola of leaves, a certain type of Virginia creeper whose name Vittoria had told me many years before but which I had forgotten.

What effect it might have on a traveller, a passenger, a customer, who got off at the wrong stop, absent-minded or sleepy, when they should have gone to Formia or Sessa Aurunca – the next stations in either direction, Formia towards Rome and Sessa towards Naples – to read PARADISO, like the funeral parlour, opposite the station, I couldn't say. I'd never happened to witness it, but I imagine it might mean crossing, going up the outside steps, reaching Paradiso, and ordering a glass of white wine. Ristorante Paradiso. You who are passing through, eager to enjoy some good food, come up and try it. That's what the marble plaque on the wall said.

We often had, on our way back from Rome or Naples. Before going home, where there wasn't always wine and we couldn't always drink. My mother would only tolerate one glass for women.

On the ground floor of two was the railwaymen's club, the place where Vittoria had spent the most time after the pharmacy.

I was looking for Gino.

Avvocato Russo, come in, that Gino's turned into a lazy so-and-so but he's usually here by nine. Would you like a coffee? An amaro? A glass of water? Although the water's not for drinking, to be honest.

Mimmo had been the stationmaster before fascism and then, since he hadn't joined the Fascist Party, he'd been sent to Cancello Arnone and demoted to points duty. Once the Fascist Party – from which we had inherited almost all of our civil service and many of its systems – had been summarily prosecuted, Mimmo had returned to his duties as stationmaster. I had never heard him, privately or in a group, utter that phrase that still echoed, that they'd been right to string Mussolini up in Piazzale Loreto. Mimmo therefore had the intransigence you find in legends.

What's Gino done, Avvocato Russo, if I may ask?

Nothing, Mimmo, why should he have?

You've taken the trouble to come all the way here, with all the work you have, and the girls. How's Luigi?

Always thinking about politics.

Eh, but not with the Party though. Oh well, you married a great man, and he married a great woman, but we're alone in this room and I don't want to embarrass you.

You flatter me, Mimmo.

So what's Gino done?

Nothing, he hasn't done anything, I wanted to ask him a few questions about Vittoria.

Eh, Avvocato Russo, I thought I'd die before her.

Why?

I'm older, I'm in a bad way, you know I've only got half a lung, don't you? And because I loved her. At least when you die you don't have to worry about things afterwards, but when someone you love dies, you do have to worry about it, and how do you fill the gap? You see that chair in the corner, avvoca'? To me it's Vittoria's, she came here every day for twenty years to thrash us at briscola. Salvatore was her partner.

Did she win?

Madonna santa, she won all right. We tried poker as well once, she practically won my pants off me.

And did she take them?

Avvocato Russo, don't ask saucy questions like that, I'm too old.

I'm sorry about Vittoria, that's why I wanted to talk to Gino.

While we're alone, avvocato, I want to tell you something, even if it's something everyone in town knows but doesn't say, or perhaps it's not true that everyone knows. But I've only got half a lung, Vittoria's dead, and you're a different generation, you've managed to get abortion, divorce, pensions for housewives, public health which my generation couldn't even imagine.

Don't say that, Mimmo, you fought the war.

And it's about that, what I wanted to say, avvoca'.

Tell me.

Do you know the story of when I was exiled to Cancello Arnone because I wouldn't join the Fascist Party?

Of course, Mimmo, you're a legend.

Well, it wasn't only because I was anti-fascist that they sent me to Cancello. It's also because I was, and still am – but only in my head nowadays – a poofter.

The word echoed so loudly in the empty room of the railwaymen's club, or only inside me, I don't know, that I pushed myself back from the table with my hands, scraping my chair along the floor, and stood up. I didn't say anything. Without looking at me, busy polishing shelves, tables, and chairs with his back still turned, Mimmo went on.

So I was lucky for a poofter too, Avvocato Russo, because a lot of them ended up much worse off. Let's be honest, avvoca', the world is full of queers, but up to a certain point you couldn't talk about it, and that had its attraction because you could still do it anyway. What I mean is, I'm not just playing down the legend thing because I've stayed in a station with only one working platform for almost twenty years, after coming from Naples where I wasn't actually a stationmaster in Mergellina, but almost. I'm trying to make you see how important Vittoria was once she came to Scauri. I saw her like those films on television, American films where everything is fine and there's music and the houses are beautiful. Vittoria came here with Mara, who looked like her daughter. Obviously, I realised straight away she wasn't her daughter, avvoca'. Vittoria got herself a boat and she kept a peacock in the garden with the cats and dogs. Paradiso wasn't that restaurant up there, Paradiso was Constantinople, that house, that life, that garden full of beautiful, scented flowers, not all of them, obviously. I've never been posh like Vittoria, you know, and it doesn't matter if it's easier for people who have no problem putting food on the table. In fact, if everyone was like Vittoria, we'd be much better off. She brought Constantinople to Scauri. Sit down, Avvocato Russo, why are you standing up? That Gino's always late, do you want a coffee?

I might as well, Mimmo, thanks.

Coming right up!

Hanging on the walls of the railwaymen's club were a faded photo of Gramsci, a recoloured picture of Berlinguer, the first page of the first issue of *L'Unità*, the first page of the first issue of *Il Manifesto*, the first page of the first issue of *La Repubblica*. On the only shelf, two cups and a trophy whose engraved plates I couldn't read, and a dangling National Partisans Association pennant. In one corner of the room was a little model railway, in working order, very detailed, with Lima carriages and wagons. The bridge looked like the Bourbon one over the Garigliano. Sleeping on the model railway, with its nose on the tunnel and its tail in the river, was the cat I had come to recognise as Gallina Nera. To the left and right of the front door, two posters: one of Termini station and the other, a night-time shot, of Naples Central. Largest of all was a map of the Italian railway network, displayed on an otherwise bare wall. While I was contemplating it, as I would contemplate the anatomical models of the vein and arterial systems in the Prince's Chapel of Sansevero in Naples, Mimmo returned with the coffee.

I didn't mean to be indiscreet, Avvocato Russo.

I never realised, Mimmo.

What is there to realise? Anyway, I would never have had Vittoria's courage. I mean, leaving her husband to live with Mara, no more security. No, I couldn't have.

Why, did you know Vittoria was married?

Yes, she told us. Look, avvocato, Gino and I and Salvatore were friends with Vittoria. Now just between us, since we're talking, I mean, who calls a cat Gallina Nera, come on! Sorry, avvoca'.

And what did Vittoria tell you, Mimmo?

That she'd fallen in love with Mara, left her job, and come here to live in Scauri.

Why Scauri?

She liked the sea, her childhood seaside.

She could have gone to Gaeta.

Vittoria said that here she wouldn't bump into so many

people she knew from Rome, they all stopped off before, at Sperlonga or Gaeta.

But I had absolutely no idea she was married, Mimmo.

Do you know how she met Mara?

No, how?

One day she went into a sock shop to buy a present for her husband, and Mara was there, selling them, and they fell in love, beautiful story, eh? Like a photo romance. Anyway it's easier for two women, avvoca'.

Easier how?

It's less disgusting for other people to imagine two women in bed. Two men, on the other hand, it's always a sin.

Do you think so?

That's what I've realised, and perhaps I agree, mine's a proper sin. Coffee's good, eh? I told you I'm Neapolitan.

Thanks, Mimmo, it's really good.

Do you know what we're going to do with Vittoria's money, avvocato? When Gino gets here I'll tell you properly, but I'll give you a hint, we're going to make it a prize for a briscola tournament and a briscola course for children. The Basile School and Prize!

But briscola's gambling.

And what's life, avvoca'? God knows when Gino'll turn up, we've all got a bit old and slow around here.

Luigi was right, the town's memory spreads out. The town's memory has a thousand intersections. The town's memory is like plants. The town's memory has roots that share information. The town's memory is inexhaustible. Time after time it's unreliable, but it's always accurate. While I was thinking about the town's memory, I tripped, dropped my bag, and put out my hands. But my elbows gave way and I fell flat on my face on the ground.

The outstretched hand ready to help me to my feet again was attached to the thin, sneering face of Filomena.

Perhaps she was sneering because it's funny to see someone fall over, perhaps because me being the one to fall made up for offending her in some way I wasn't aware of, or because it just gave her some small, miserable satisfaction. After all, we'd never liked each other, even at school.

I think she hated me because I was better at school, and cleaner, although we came from the same street.

I think her mother hated mine because she tried to hide the dirt. After all, as my mother said – and it's one of the few things I think she's right about – being posh means the certainty that you can't be bought or that money buys everything.

Filomena's mother, meanwhile, acted poor, as they say around here. She acted poor at the Immacolata, where the Brothers tried to help everyone. She acted poorer and poorer down at Sant'Albina, with Father Salvatore, who calmly tried to get her to think about the many others in the town who were worse off than she was, along with very many others around the world. She also tried it on when Father Salvatore was succeeded by Father Michele, but more half-heartedly, because by then the funeral parlour had opened.

In Filomena's house they went around dressed in tatters. And that lasted until a certain point when Filomena and I were both beginning middle school, but no longer in the same class, and her father expanded the Paradiso funeral parlour with sudden, unexpected funds. A nice shop in the centre, and no longer a hole in the wall at the cemetery.

From then on, since death is a sure-fire investment, Filomena, her mother, and her brother – whose name is either Vittore or Filippo, no one knows which – were better if not tastefully dressed, or perhaps with the taste of that period, i.e. designer clothes they bought in Formia.

Designer clothes age quickly, for which reason my mother bought us second-hand clothes, and it wasn't only a question of money: with second-hand clothes you could always say they were handed down from relatives, they were too big or too small. With second-hand clothes you can invent stories about wealthy relatives you don't have. Anyway, Filomena helped me to my feet. She said Sit down a minute, you've had a nasty knock.

We sat in the doorway of a house where no one lived, which had been for sale for a couple of years.

Do you reckon they can't sell it because the price is too high?

I'm only concerned with people's final homes, Le'. I don't know about the ones before and I'm not interested.

She held out a bottle of water to me and a man's cotton handkerchief. I took both without much enthusiasm. VITTORIA was embroidered on the handkerchief.

Filome', what have you got to do with those two?

What have *you* got to do with them? You think you're more important than me because you went to university?

No, I've got nothing to do with them either, but Vittoria involved me, she told Father Michele to give me her will.

Yes, but what have you got to do with them as a person, not as a lawyer? You hardly even came to their house.

That's not true, I used to drop by.

Yes, you dropped by, but you never stayed.

I've got two little girls.

So what? You could have brought them.

Where?

To Mara and Vittoria's house.

I felt embarrassed.

Why?

Well, two women living together, not mother and daughter, with that age difference. Silvia and I are closer in age than they are.

But they weren't mother and daughter, Le'.

I know, but why are you always with Mara then, Filomena?

I'm not sure whether I don't know how to tell you or I don't want to tell you, but first you answer a question. All this superiority of yours, what's that about?

Sitting at my desk, I looked at the document folders and pretended to think about work, but really I was concentrating on the keyhole, trying to figure out what Cristina was doing in the other room. I hated her because she hadn't been to

Registri Buffetti and I needed stationery. And in the morning she'd bought ripe bananas whose smell impregnated the whole office.

My head hurt and a purple bump was growing on my forehead.

What do secretaries do when no one's watching? I couldn't tell and so I imagined, like I suppose blind and deaf people do.

But I wasn't blind, my ears were frustrated by what they weren't used to deducing from sounds, so at half twelve, when it was reasonable for me to go out for lunch, I went. I might have said See you in a bit, I might have said nothing. I'd thought I'd be able to learn the subject of the letter from the clicking of the keys on the typewriter. I had failed.

Once out, I took the road alongside Ernesto Bruno towards the seafront. Carmela was cleaning the windows, but she didn't see me. I turned left, and although I felt like running I just walked faster. A few metres from the liceo scientifico I heard the bell, hurried, and reached the car park in front of the school, an old convent whose windows overlooked the sea.

On Mondays Luigi taught the final period.

I followed him as he came out of the front door, surrounded by girls from the fourth and fifth years, beautiful, young, light: they seemed free of doubts to me and therefore successful. Did he like those animated, darting girls, who walked backwards to keep talking to him? Or was he like gynaecologists, who've had enough after a while? Had he had enough of youth?

I went to a gynaecologist, not frequently. I didn't like gynaecologists or dentists. Who does? Luigi would ask in that teasing tone of his. He looked up from the students and smiled at me, unsurprised, perhaps he was expecting me. He must have said something, because the girls all looked at me as one. They were so beautiful. Perhaps I was the one who liked those girls, not him. Since Vittoria died, I was confused. Filomena was right, who did I think I was? This superiority of yours, Le', what's that about?

Where shall we go and eat?

Shall we see if L'Arenauta's open?

All the way down there! It's almost in Sperlonga!

Well, Paola's at home with the girls. I'll tell her you're not coming back.

Luigi went back inside to phone. Since he was no longer available, the students gathered around me.

Avvocato.

Good morning, girls.

How did you manage to get Riccardo all that money?

The question caught me off guard. A petite blonde girl had stepped forward, one green lock of hair and black nails, very thin, a punky Parmigianino.

Saturday night, on the beach, they were fighting because of me, but Riccardo's a dickhead, avvocato, you shouldn't have got him that money, he's boasting about it everywhere like he won it in the lottery. At least he won't be stealing wafers from the church any more to get some cash.

Why were they fighting?

Because I fancied Antonello.

Are you and Riccardo together?

What if we are, avvoca'? What's that got to do with it? It's not like someone can harass you because you fancy someone else.

That's not what I'm saying, or what I think.

Antonello came over to see me, we met in summer when he was on holiday and he met Vittoria, so he stayed a bit longer.

Where does Vittoria come into it?

Vittoria's sort of Antonello's aunt.

Did you know Vittoria was married?

No, I found out at the funeral. Anyway, when you call someone aunt they're not necessarily related.

No. But what did Antonello want with Vittoria?

To meet her.

Why?

He was curious, he recognised her on the seafront from a photo at his grandma's brother's house, and then at the funeral I realised Antonello's uncle was Vittoria's husband and the lawyer defending him as well.

What did Vittoria and Antonello talk about?

How should I know, avvoca', I didn't ask him all these questions, did I? I'll give you his number if you want and you can ask him. But why did that dickhead get all that money?

What do you think about Riccardo then?

That he'll blow all that money with those guys he was selling the wafers to, telling them they're blessed, and those bastards believe it, but maybe that crap about the wafers is over now.

Luigi and I didn't talk in the car, we sang along to Battiato on the radio and enjoyed the bends, which in his Renault 4 always provided a certain thrill.

Passano ancora lenti i treni per Tozeur, ta ta ta ta ta.

L'Arenauta was closed, so we turned back towards Gaeta and, at the end of the port, we stopped under the pergola of Il Francese. I liked restaurants with pergolas.

So how's this Vittoria business coming along?

It's getting complicated.

You're getting complicated, Lea.

No, Luigi, I'm not getting complicated, but I'm involved and I don't know why.

Shall I tell you?

Do you know?

No, I don't, but I've thought about it.

And?

You don't like not knowing things that are going on around you, you don't like thinking that you've hung out with or even bumped into someone for twenty years and never even imagined anything more than what you saw, and we all saw, so you're not the only one, but you feel stupid.

The old men at the railway club knew she was married.

So the old men knew, Lea.

It's not just that I didn't know much about her, Luigi. It's that the little I did know was wrong.

The wind ruffled the leaves of the pergola, spreading the sound of rustling fabric into the air. A scooter screeched to a halt and the whistle of the brakes was followed by swearing. Turning in the direction of the voice that had taken first God's and then Our Lady's name in vain, I focused on the delicate nape of Luigi's neck, with the elongated hairline that had been passed on intact to Silvia's head, like a photocopy. I couldn't tell whether I loved him because I often looked at him close up, or I looked at him close up because I loved him.

But what if the fact that I can't stand not knowing, my feeling stupid, as you put it, has nothing to do with it? What if I've realised that I wanted to be with her?

Lea, take it from your husband, you don't fancy women.

He leaned in to kiss me, I turned my head away.

All right, you fancied Vittoria, choose the simple version, it's fine by me, it's your life, but part of your life is mine, so listen to me.

I asked for a light, I couldn't do anything else.

What does it mean, that you like someone, Le'? It's nothing, saying you like someone means you want to be near them, a level of closeness, but when you get close you can see what they have around them, and it's that context, or whatever you want to call it, that you like, in the end. That's why it's easy to fall in love but loving is complicated, because often you don't just like the things around the person you think you're in love with, you also like the people they're close to, it's difficult, it's a kind of force field.

What does that mean?

It's like an electrical field or a magnetic field.

So?

It's not called a force crowd but a force field, because it's a feature of space, and love is a feature of space too. A person, where they live, who they have around them.

What are you saying, Luigi?

That I also fell in love with you for your family, for example. While I've never liked your mother.

What happened to your head?

I tripped over, but it's getting better.

Filomena's version was simple: she was giving Mara a hand because Vittoria had helped her father, and she had a good memory. Although her father said that didn't happen, he won the money playing cards, without cheating.

But the truth that everyone knew and that Lino, Filomena's father, wanted to ignore, was that in over twenty years Vittoria had only lost one match – that one – and that one person's bad luck should so greatly favour, indeed coincide with another person's good luck, is rare, even impossible. A fairy tale. On the other hand, a certain sum might be a fortune to so-and-so, while the same sum is nothing much to someone else. I thought about Vittoria. Had it cost her more to lose or to pay?

Are you sure, Filomena?

My father didn't know how to play cards, Le', while Vittoria was used to playing with people's lives.

What does that mean?

Oh, you're always on about what things mean. It means that someone does something good for others to clear their conscience.

I don't understand.

What, you start living with someone who could be your daughter, and you don't realise at a certain point that it was wrong, and so you have to make up for it?

I believe Mara was a consenting adult.

What if it was an old guy with a young girl, would you say the same or would you say he was disgusting?

I don't know, it depends on the situation. You can't generalise, there's no rule.

Mara was led astray, Lea, did you know Vittoria was the first woman she'd been with?

And also the last, do you think, Filome'?

It's no use looking at me like that, like you're insinuating something, and I'm not saying Mara doesn't fancy me, and she hasn't thought about it, and doesn't think about it, because she's been led astray now, but me, I like cock.

In the afternoon, incited by Paola, who evidently thought she had to go to lunch with Luigi, the girls demanded the story of the old man and the old woman with the old beans. When they'd started doing their homework I told Luigi what I'd come up with.

The Vittoria affair was starting to seem like an exercise in Greek prose, or Greek itself. If I'd been born into a different family I might have studied Latin and Greek at university, but I felt I had to get my parents away from the land, try and buy them the house where they had been labourers for thirty years, and the legal profession seemed quicker to me than teaching, even though I'd always enjoyed studying.

Vittoria was like Greek. She had left few clues, and to reach a meaning, if there was one, you had to proceed by rearranging all the elements, knowing there would always be a margin of interpretation left, or in the worst case that none of the rearrangements would make sense.

Luigi was more upset by the news that Vittoria had killed herself than by the violence Mara had been subjected to.

You said Mara was a tart.

What does that mean? Does it make it less serious?

No, but.

It was a puzzle. Not what the truth is, but when the truth is. When a thing is true and when it stops being true, or when it's false and becomes true. Basically, the truth is worthless compared to time.

But why would someone like that kill herself? wondered Luigi, standing up and adding, I'm going out to the garden a minute. Then he stopped and looked me in the eyes, and said You can't judge anyone for their fears, so if Vittoria was afraid of pain, she was right to do what she did. Once, many years ago, I'd come to Scauri on leave for two days, I wanted to come and see you, we were just engaged. At the station I met Vittoria and we walked the road down to the sea together. I would have taken the Appia, but I followed Vittoria because she started talking to me about you.

I remembered the other night, when you said Vittoria might have fancied you, and I said Don't be silly, but then I remembered that walk.

What did she say to you?

She asked me what our life was like as young graduates in a little town where hardly anyone had a degree, and how I felt being engaged to a woman who wouldn't be a housewife and might, almost certainly would, earn more than me. Imagine being asked those questions. I was twenty-five. I said Not all intelligent men marry stupid women, or something like that, and I might have asked after Mara and she answered that they were fine, and nothing more, and that she was happy Mara had found something that suited her in Scauri, she had always liked animals. She smiled, I might not remember her words but her smile I do. So when I remembered that walk I wondered whether, when Vittoria used the word animals, she might have meant us too. I thought about it again the other evening. We were walking and I was looking at the ground, I was intimidated, I don't know why, only I'm tall and I realised I was looking down on her, and out of geometrical confidence I plucked up my courage and asked her if she'd ever wanted to be a man.

And what did she say?

She said yes, she said she'd realised that in Mexico.

So you knew she'd been to Mexico.

But that's not the point. I wanted to tell her she was a lesbian, I wanted to offend her.

You're exactly like that bastard Riccardo.

I was young and then she'd told me you'd earn more than me, she'd practically called me a half-man.

Being young is no justification for being stupid. Anyway, why did Vittoria want to be a man in Mexico?

She thought that if Mexico had still been undiscovered, she couldn't have been a captain or a sailor on the exploration, so she would have liked to be a man. She felt more suited to external adventures than internal ones, that's what she told me.

Perfect, Luigi, but now help me figure this out: do you think someone like that kills herself because she's afraid of pain?

I'm going out into the garden for a bit, he repeated.

Despite never turning up at the railwaymen's club that morning for some reason to do with Gallina Nera, a brome grass seed in his ear, someone must have told Gino I was looking for him and that the missing cat was there at the club. His version of events was simple, and as he talked he sounded like Suetonius. Suetonius as described at school, because apart from a few excerpts in translation class, I'd never read him.

Avvoca', I was at that match, I was. Lino, that cheapskate from up the hill, he told her, If I beat you at poker you lend me the money, and all of us who were there, we lit ourselves a cigarette. I don't know if you've ever seen Stalin's musicals, avvoca', perhaps not, because you're too young.

No, I haven't.

Well, we saw them.
Musicals?
Yes, ballets.
Ballets?

Yes, Joseph Stalin liked ballets, anyway, I don't want to waste your time, avvoca', I'm retired but you're not. Anyway, we lit a cigarette together like a dance company in a Joseph Stalin musical. Vittoria never lost at poker, avvoca', can you believe it? Never, so there was nothing to be done. We looked at Lino with our eyes wide to make him stop, but it was no use, he's an idiot. Then Vittoria said she didn't lend money, she wasn't a cravattara. Which is a word I didn't know. Then Mimmo, who'd been to Rome – before all that stuff about being anti-fascist and unnatural, if I may say so, I don't know what you think, avvoca', but it's different for women – anyway, Mimmo said that cravattara means moneylender.

So how did the money business end up?

Vittoria says Let's play for that amount, if you win it you win it, if you lose you lose. But if I lose I can't pay you, Lino snaps back. Then you'll give me the land, Vittoria explains, shuffling the cards. I don't know if you ever saw her play, avvoca', but the way she shuffled. And she knew some games I'd never seen, too, she liked briscola more than poker and more than scopone, she was really good at tressette. She didn't lose much at all, at poker never, except that time, which is why I think – in fact I'm sure, since Lino wasn't up to much in life, never mind at cards – that Vittoria let him win. The funeral parlour might be the one good idea Lino ever had, and he could have had it earlier, since he comes from generations of gravediggers.

Really.

Lino's grandad was at the cemetery too.

Well, Gino, we'll all be at the cemetery sooner or later.

Better later, avvoca', trust me.

Mara's gate was open, so my arrival went unannounced by its creak and I rang the bell. It had started to rain but the patio was sheltered. An opaque, sleepy sheen seemed to have descended on the garden. I was sleepy too, it must have been the change of seasons, or the wine. The pinky-white bellflowers on the carport were wilting, the berries were turning from red to burgundy and purply-red, for the first time the leaves were yellowing on the cobblestones, and the roses seemed to have broken free, or to have wanted to, from the clamp in which Vittoria had locked them so many years before. Are bushes ugly?

I'd never realised how much effort had gone into maintaining the garden like that. A dance company, as Gino had said. Each with their role, each in their place. The will, work, patience, effort, and forcefulness too, I thought, looking at a dog rose which was attempting to escape the column Vittoria had forced it to climb. Omnipotence is exerted by gardeners. Working day after day, year after year, to freeze life, growing and rotting, in one image. All renewed, all the same.

The wind had carried a few leaves onto the little iron table around which were two chairs, also iron, that might have been repainted every summer. They were showing their age and what they were made of, both things a good coat of paint will hide. A conversation with Vittoria returned like an echo. There had been the same buzzing sound I could hear now from the house next door, which seemed empty, as it had then. Not buzzing, a piece of machinery running, a rumble and a squeak, nothing sinister, just annoying. It came in waves, depending on the wind. Same as the other time.

It might have been three in the afternoon. We were sitting at the little table, the chairs weren't white back then but sage green. I don't remember what we were talking about, but at a certain point we started wondering about that continuous, persistent noise. Where it was coming from. I said perhaps someone was cooking, Vittoria said no, it was no longer or not yet time to eat, they were probably checking that some household appliance worked. Then a dark-haired girl came out and smiled at us, holding a bowl of murky water. What's that noise? asked Vittoria, in a tone somewhere between curiosity and annoyance, both sincere. They're making mayonnaise, answered the girl, disconsolately, there's a party tomorrow. So at some point it'll stop, Vittoria went on, sweetly. Embarrassed, I tried to joke about it. Isn't it something that loses it if you're too rough with it? I'll go and tell them to stop, said the dark girl, relieved. No, don't, if it doesn't bother you, don't worry, we're fine, Vittoria insisted, persuasively, even more than persuasively, seductively perhaps. Vittoria smiled at me, I smiled back, and shortly afterwards, a sharp whistle anticipated the silence. The grinding noise had stopped.

The dark girl came out on the balcony raising her thumb. Vittoria managed to get silence without even asking for it.

In the opaque afternoon, enveloped by that buzzing that reminded me of another, I sat down to take in the garden. How much determination had it taken to bend the plants in that particular way so they created a sensation of peace and naturalness, expressed beauty, or how much care, without cruelty. Is care good or bad? Drugs and poison. Proportion. Constantinople.

I'd seen an interview with Carla Fracci on television after a first night at La Scala or the San Carlo, I don't remember, some theatre. My daughters dreamed of wearing pink tutus, but they were too undisciplined. Carla Fracci was exhorting people to dance, a kind of admonition that went beyond dance and became part of daily life. Silvia and Giulia were quivering, glued to the television, and I thought that dance and daily life, as ritual and discipline, single and collective, can be superimposed, one taking the shape of the other. Carla Fracci said, calmly, When you think about the lightness of ballet dancers, look at their feet. Dancers' feet retain the memory of all the exercises, all the efforts, all the weight, all the significance of repetitions, balance, jumps, the effort of fixing life, which is movement, in an eternal and eternally recognisable geometric shape. Looking at Vittoria's garden,

I wondered where that dark and knotty place was, hidden, deformed by exercise and balance, that, however, guaranteed lightness and grace, or the semblance of them.

So can ballerinas wear all the colours then, Mamma? asked Silvia, taking her hand off the screen with the consequent electrostatic crackle of hair.

A noise of claws distracted me and Gallina Nera appeared, rolling a knobbly seed head with his paw so it made a noise like maracas. Claws and rain sticks. Abacuses. Rice poured into a glass jar. Behind the cat, as if drawn there by an invisible thread, came Mara. She wasn't surprised to see me. Swaying, she leaned on the table.

You're always drunk.

What do you expect me to do, Lea? The rabbits are dead and the cat's playing with the jimson weed seeds on the dryer.

Isn't that poisonous?

Not for cats, only for humans, but there are plenty of poisonous plants in the garden to go round.

Why, though?

Vittoria made medicines, Lea, remember.

I smoked one, two, three, four cigarettes, then Mara said It's cold, let's go inside.

She made a herbal tea and put a plate of chocolate biscuits in front of me. I loved chocolate biscuits.

Before I tell you something, I want to show you a lovely figurine.

She was laughing and swaying but I wasn't, I was just worried. I don't like drunks.

Vittoria dried jimson weed seeds and planted poisonous herbs and flowers.

Mara came back with a little Limoges figurine. A girl holding a basket of flowers. It was exquisitely made, the skin fair and rosy, pale-blue ribbons on the dress and tying the flowers.

This figurine was on Vittoria's bedside table in her bedroom in the Rome house, where she lived with the lawyer you met. I went there one evening, for a party. I wasn't even eighteen but I told everyone I was nearly twenty-three. He was drunk, I didn't want to, he was good-looking, he was violent. After all, I was a paid guest.

What does that mean?

What you think it does. I was paid to go to parties, extra for sex. It was a beautiful house, I'd never been in such a beautiful house, there were elegant people. Vittoria was there, but I only looked at her properly when he opened the door again. I was half-naked, I wanted to leave, I was embarrassed to be so dishevelled in front of such a beautiful woman but I saw the figurine, the figurine was so beautiful too, it still is. I felt like this little porcelain girl who certainly cost more than I did. It was a vain thought, Vittoria told me the only time we talked about it, a long time later. That evening, on the floor, with my dress torn, I thought that the figurine wasn't broken and neither was I. It was something my mum used to say, or my grandma, or perhaps it's something every poor soul says to remind themselves they'll be okay. I don't think

I'd thought all these things then, but with Vittoria I didn't just learn words, I learned how to use them. I'll never really be like you and her, but I'm a bit like you.

There is no me and her.

Yes there is, Lea, but you can't see it.

What happened that evening though?

Vittoria gave me the figurine and said From now on I'll take care of you.

And then?

She took care of me.

Did you fancy her though?

Yes, I did. I didn't realise straight away that she wanted to leave Rome, leave her job at the university and all the rest, I didn't want her to do that for me, it seemed like too much.

But?

She told me she would have done it anyway, and if it hadn't been me it would have been someone else.

Do you believe that?

Who knows. At a certain point I said yes, and we came to Scauri, she said I amused her, I deserved a lighter life.

And what about her husband, her job?

I don't know. I think she went to Rome a few times. At the beginning she used to go, and come back with postcards and souvenirs like a tourist. She wouldn't say anything. She brought back the plaster head.

And you never asked?

She didn't like answering questions, she hardly ever told me anything.

But you were attracted to her?
I think I could have got married and had kids.
You still can, you're young.
No, I don't think being young comes into it.
What, then?
My body's got the habit now, we all get habits, think about those people who come here every evening for a beer, Vittoria swimming every morning, or you always buying pastries at Vezza's or Morelli's, your pants from Ernesto Bruno, pizza from Lu Rusticone. I mean, why should love be different from any of that?

Which one is jimson weed? I don't know it.

The large bellflowers, near the carport, the white and pink ones. I'm going for a rest now, I don't know if I'm going to be okay, Vittoria's always been here. The garden was enveloped in a violent peace. Those bellflowers are so beautiful, even though they're wilting now. They're fatal, you know. Vittoria said you just had to fall asleep under them, but you actually have to eat them.

How many?

I don't know, I was never the one taking care of the plants. In the end I'd rather let them do what they want. Let them at least do what they want.

In the late afternoon, the Via Appia was teeming with people running around to get their last bits of shopping. As if Sundays lasted a month. They replenished their stores. Luigi and I liked to think that since the average age of the town was high, the memory of the postwar period, the hunger lingered. I wondered whether Mara knew about Vittoria's illness, whether it was right to talk to her about it. I answered myself that despite what Rebecca had said, if Vittoria hadn't told her, it wasn't my place to.

I got into the car with the bag from the butcher's in one hand and a sack of potatoes in the other. I wanted to make cutlets for the girls. And chips. I'd also bought two pig's livers. Luigi didn't eat offal, and perhaps because he was used to his mum's cooking, he only liked well-cooked cutlets.

On the seafront the beach clubs glowed in the golden sunset. Every time I watched the sun set into the water, I would think that all you need to do to be beautiful is to set. Then I thought of Silvia and Giulia, and I knew they were beautiful, and I didn't want them to set at all. Young couples strolled along, entwined around each other. Two women in chenille jogging suits were walking briskly. One of them was Anna, Riccardo's mum, and the other was the English teacher who lived near Vittoria and Mara.

The plaster on the houses tried to withstand the salty sea air. Dance music was coming from La Bussola, and the men were smoking and drinking beer, holding in their bellies. The lights were on in two of the rooms at Villa Eleonora, Scauri's only hotel. The curtains were open in one room, not in the other. In front of Lido Delfini three men were playing bocce.

*

The last person I would have expected to see at Lo Scoglio was Avvocato Pontecorvo, sitting at my table. Tobia gave me a questioning look. I shrugged, brusquely. Give me a beer then, I said, still looking in the direction of the lawyer. How long's he been here?

A couple of hours, he's barely stopped looking out of the window.

What did he have?

Just water.

I took my beer, sipped it, and when I reached the table sat down opposite Pontecorvo.

Can I offer you a beer?

No thank you, Lea.

I thought you said you'd never set foot in Scauri again?

I came to cover the cost of the boat.

It's not your problem.

I asked them not to say anything, and I hope you won't either.

You ought to analyse your fondness for the relationship between money and silence.

It's nothing unusual, Avvocato Russo, people have paid for silence since time immemorial. Or are you dabbling in psychology now?

No, Avvocato Pontecorvo, I'm not. I simply notice repetitions, recurrences, it's part of the profession, isn't it?

Anyway, I was waiting for you.

Why?

I've always been curious, as Vittoria was, about people who are certain they are somehow morally superior.

You're wrong about me, I don't think I'm morally superior at all.

Do you think so, Avvocato Russo? Do you know yourself that well? How admirable.

I have to go home to my daughters now, so I'll say goodbye, Avvocato Pontecorvo.

Bon appétit, my dear Lea.

It was St Stephen's Day many years before, I wasn't yet married. We'd gone to play cards, backgammon, bocce too, in the living room, on the carpet, something so exotic no one had ever dreamed of suggesting it, but anything was possible at Constantinople. Playing bocce on the carpet. Carpets, too. Carpets created dust more than anything else. Now I knew about the parties in Rome, I thought about how different the rooms and people were. Perhaps Vittoria enjoyed herself anyway. Here and there, the queen of the party. That evening, when I was about to say something, Vittoria put her hand over my mouth and pulled me towards her. I felt her breasts against my back, and she repeated, happily, Don't say anything, don't say anything. In the end, she said the thing I wasn't to say, which was about her. She had pinched two little plants from Patella after arguing about the best way to grow capers. I should have asked Tommaso if you can kill yourself with jimson weed, with nightshade, with who knows what. The wrong spinach leaves.

At home the phone was ringing. I put down my bags and lifted the receiver, still calling out Where are you all? and turning my head this way and that, with no reply. The girls must have gone somewhere with Luigi. Alba was on the phone. The sphinx cat she bought for her daughter had been kidnapped. I swear, Lea, she said, I'm not paying a lira if they ask for a ransom.

Down in the garden, two pigeons pecking at the gravel looked like mice to me.

NOTE

Scauri exists. It's the town in the province of Latina where I was born and raised. The businesses and beach clubs exist, or did. Gisella Treglia was brutally murdered in the pinewoods at Marina di Minturno, my sisters are called Silvia and Giulia, Russo is my mother's surname, my father is a physicist, Luigi was my paternal grandfather's name. My grandmother's family surname is Nocella. Linona ("Big Lina") is the nickname of Lina Tammaro, a great friend of my parents, but she's not a pharmacist. The surnames mentioned are on the doorbells in Scauri; no one in the book refers to the people who have those surnames. Tobia runs Lo Scoglio, under Monte d'Oro. The story of the drunk children biting the rabbits' ears was told to me by Antonella Ingletto, one summer in Marittima, in Lecce province. Daria Corrias told me about the midwife who can birth breech babies without needing a Caesarean; it was her mother, Sebastiana, who worked in Nuoro. Vittoria, Lea, Rebecca, Pontecorvo, the railwaymen do not exist; no one exists. Perhaps even I don't exist. But I listen to stories about people I know and don't know and I weave them together. The stories do exist, somewhere. They're echoes, sometimes tributes, nothing more, there's no accuracy or reporting, it's all mixed up, misunderstood, invented, lies.

Il Golfo is a monthly paper that has just celebrated its fiftieth anniversary. It comes out almost every month but has nothing to do with the parishes of the Immacolata or Sant'Albina. It is edited by Damiano Pontecorvo, who, despite sharing a surname with him, has no connection, relationship, or anything else to do with the lawyer in the book: he is a historian and journalist. Which reminds me: my parents always subscribed to *Il Golfo*.

I had the idea for this short novel a few years ago, when I was adapting *Le grand Bob* by Georges Simenon for *Ad alta voce* on RAI Radio 3, and it came back to me when my friends Ena Marchi and Giorgio Pinotti invited me to an event celebrating an anniversary of the author, whose work is published by Adelphi in Italy. I was asked to talk about female figures in the non-Maigret novels of Simenon, and since my dear Ena and Giorgio are so kind, precise, and well prepared, they sent me a certain number of them. More than twenty-five. What did I realise about female figures in Simenon's novels? Let's leave that heart-rending question unanswered. *The Little I Knew* (*Chi dice e chi tace* in Italian) was almost entirely written in the summer of 2021, with the title *Dopo il funerale*, while I was writing *Così per sempre* (Einaudi, 2022), but then Michela died.

"She knew earthly plants better than heavenly ones" is from Plato's *Timaeus* ("Humans are not an earthly plant but a heavenly one"). "There is infinite hope, but not for us" is Kafka in *Letters to Milena*. "The old insidious habit" is from *Revolutionary Road* by Richard Yates ("From old, insidious habit"). "Enveloped in a violent peace" is by Fleur Jaeggy in the story "Agnes" from *I Am the Brother of XX*. And that's all I remember. So aside from the things mentioned here, there remain those unsaid or forgotten.

This book is dedicated to the memory of Carmen Rosati, who died while stationary at traffic lights the summer after she left school. She was my friend, and *una bella capa fresca*, an airhead, generous and fun, so much so that she contradicted the edict of Saint-Cloud, according to which the dead must stay out of the way of the living. The traffic lights where Carmen died have been made into a roundabout, and I still drive that way. Carmen knew, as all of us born in the province know, that the dead are in the way.

And it's for Dafni Scotese as well, who also died while I was revising these pages, in a road accident, on a bend between Minturno and Scauri, and contradicted the edict of Saint-Cloud too. The dead are in the way.

This novel is for my nephews, Francesco and Angelo Rosso, that they may never throw bottles, and that they may look and look again and manage to enjoy the provinces.

And it's for Marcella.

Gallina Nera is obviously Miles. The grass seed in the ear is his too.

Foundry Editions
40 Randolph Street
London NW1 0SR
United Kingdom

First published in 2024 as *Chi dice e chi tace* by Chiara Valerio, © 2024 Sellerio Editore, Palermo

Translation © Ailsa Wood 2025

This first edition published by Foundry Editions in 2025

The moral right of Chiara Valerio to be identified as the Author of this work has been asserted in accordance with the Copyright, Designs and Patents Act 1988.

A CIP record for this title is available from the British Library.

ISBN 978-1-0686934-8-9

Series cover design by Murmurs Design
Designed and typeset in LfA Aluminia by Tetragon, London
Printed and bound by TJ Books, Padstow, Cornwall

All rights reserved. No part of this publication may be reproduced, stored in a retrieval system or transmitted in any form or by any means, electronic, mechanical, photocopying, recording or otherwise, without prior permission in writing from Foundry Editions.

foundryeditions.co.uk

EU GPSR authorised representative: Logos Europe, 9 rue Nicolas Poussin, 17000 La Rochelle, France; contact@logoseurope.eu.

FOUNDRY EDITIONS

1 CONSTANTIA SOTERIOU (CYPRUS)
Brandy Sour
tr. from Greek by Lina Protopapa

2 MARIA GRAZIA CALANDRONE (ITALY)
Your Little Matter
tr. from Italian by Antonella Lettieri

3 ROSA RIBAS (SPAIN)
Far
tr. from Spanish by Charlotte Coombe

4 ABDELAZIZ BARAKA SAKIN (SUDAN)
Samahani
tr. from Arabic by Mayada Ibrahim and Adil Babikir

5 ESTHER GARCÍA LLOVET (SPAIN)
Spanish Beauty
tr. from Spanish by Richard Village

6 KARIM KATTAN (PALESTINE)
The Palace on the Higher Hill
tr. from French by Jeffrey Zuckerman

7 CÉCILE TLILI (FRANCE)
Just a Little Dinner
tr. from French by Katherine Gregor

8 CHIARA VALERIO (ITALY)
The Little I Knew
tr. from Italian by Ailsa Wood

9 ANNA PAZOS (SPAIN/CATALONIA)
Killing the Nerve
tr. from Catalan by Charlotte Coombe and Laura McGloughlin

10 MATTEO MELCHIORRE (ITALY)
The Duke
tr. from Italian by Antonella Lettieri